SPOOK

THE HALLOWEEN CAT

BY Dean Norman

STAR BRIGHT BOOKS
CAMBRIDGE, MASSACHUSETTS

Published by Star Bright Books in 2015

Published in the United States of America by Star Bright Books, Inc.
The name Star Bright Books and the Star Bright Books logo are registered trademarks of Star Bright Books, Inc. Please visit: www.starbrightbooks.com.
For bulk orders, please email: orders@starbrightbooks.com, or
call customer service at: (617) 354-1300.

Printed on paper from sustainable forests

ISBN-13: 978-1-59572-709-1
Star Bright Books / MA / 00108150
Printed in Canada / Marquis / 0 9 8 7 6 5 4 3 2 1

Library of Congress Cataloging-in-Publication Data is available.

Dedicated to a black kitten I got from the
Cleveland Animal Protective League— D.N.

MEOW MEOW
MEOW

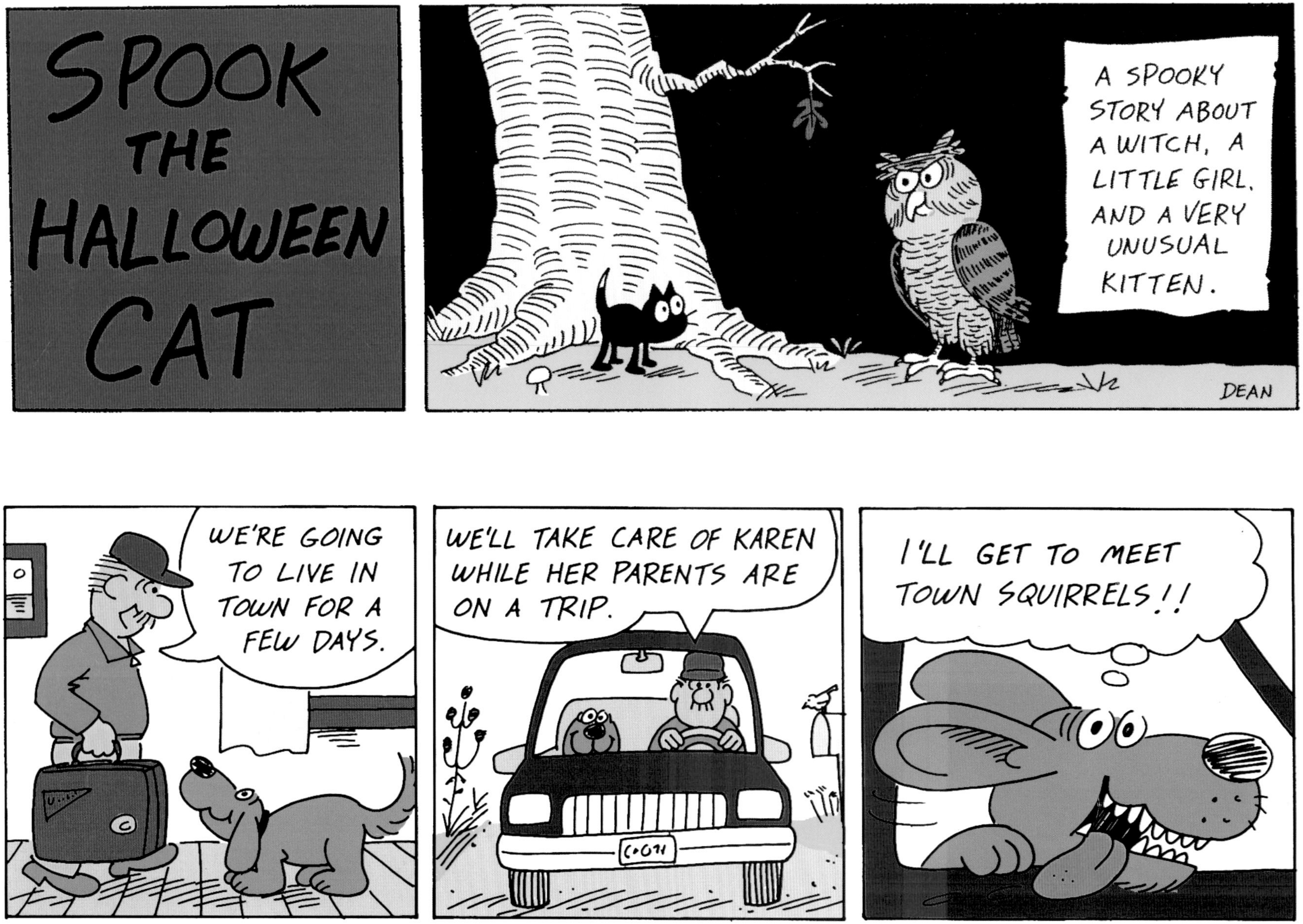
SPOOK THE HALLOWEEN CAT
A SPOOKY STORY ABOUT A WITCH, A LITTLE GIRL, AND A VERY UNUSUAL KITTEN.
DEAN
WE'RE GOING TO LIVE IN TOWN FOR A FEW DAYS.
WE'LL TAKE CARE OF KAREN WHILE HER PARENTS ARE ON A TRIP.
I'LL GET TO MEET TOWN SQUIRRELS!!

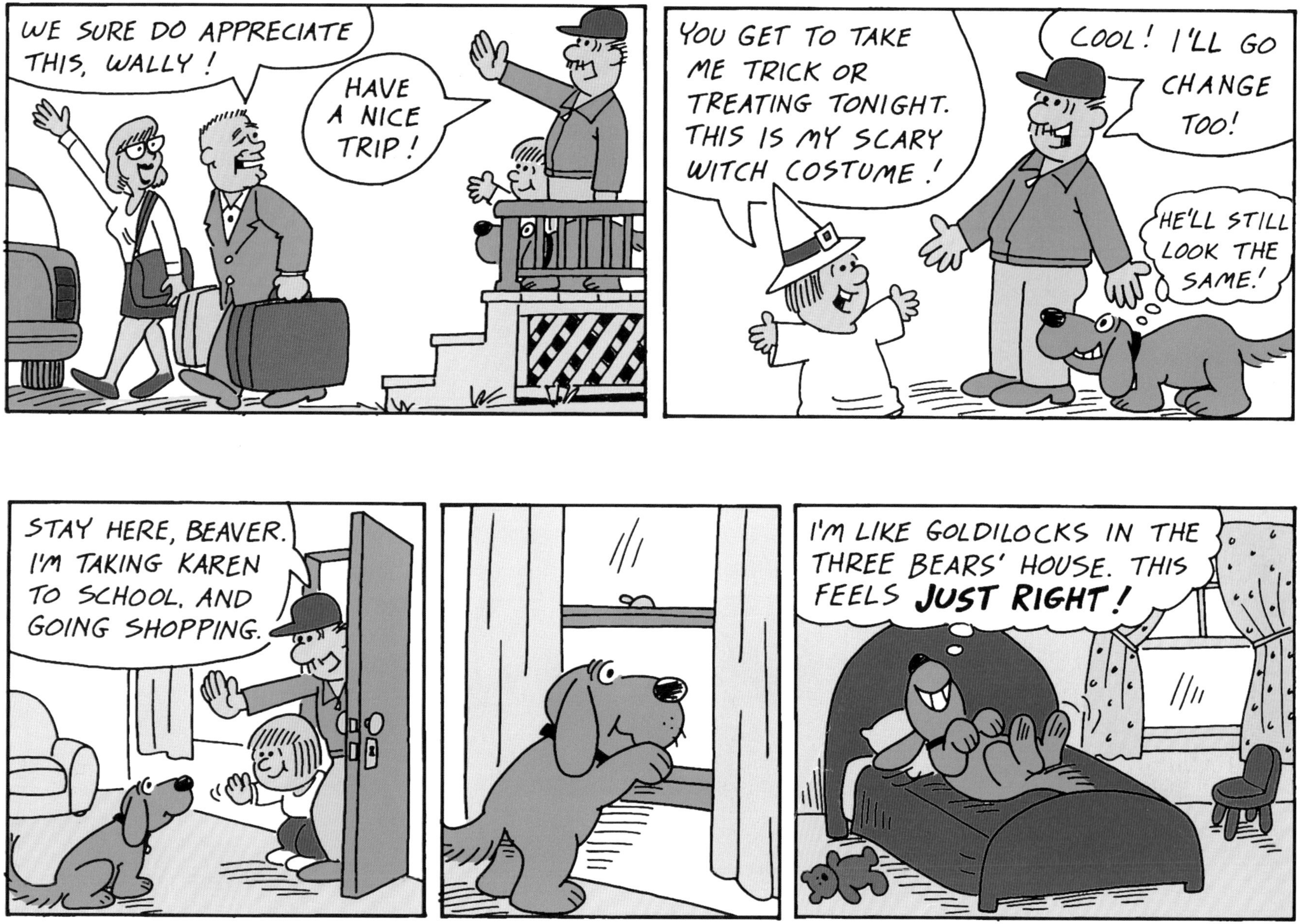
WE SURE DO APPRECIATE THIS, WALLY!
HAVE A NICE TRIP!
YOU GET TO TAKE ME TRICK OR TREATING TONIGHT. THIS IS MY SCARY WITCH COSTUME!
COOL! I'LL GO CHANGE TOO!
HE'LL STILL LOOK THE SAME!
STAY HERE, BEAVER. I'M TAKING KAREN TO SCHOOL. AND GOING SHOPPING.
I'M LIKE GOLDILOCKS IN THE THREE BEARS' HOUSE. THIS FEELS **JUST RIGHT**!

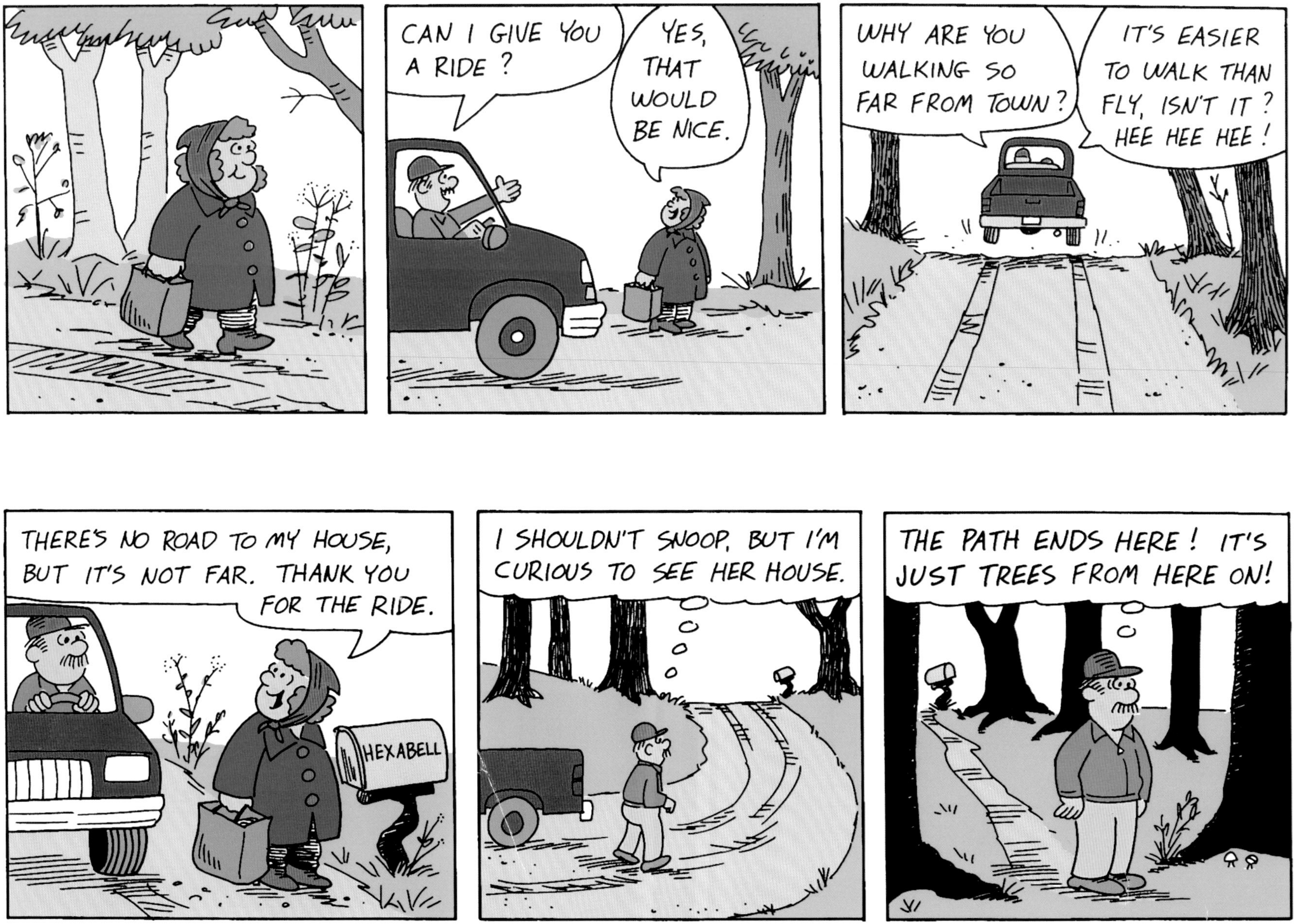
CAN I GIVE YOU A RIDE?
YES, THAT WOULD BE NICE.
WHY ARE YOU WALKING SO FAR FROM TOWN?
IT'S EASIER TO WALK THAN FLY, ISN'T IT? HEE HEE HEE!
THERE'S NO ROAD TO MY HOUSE, BUT IT'S NOT FAR. THANK YOU FOR THE RIDE.
HEXABELL
I SHOULDN'T SNOOP, BUT I'M CURIOUS TO SEE HER HOUSE.
THE PATH ENDS HERE! IT'S JUST TREES FROM HERE ON!

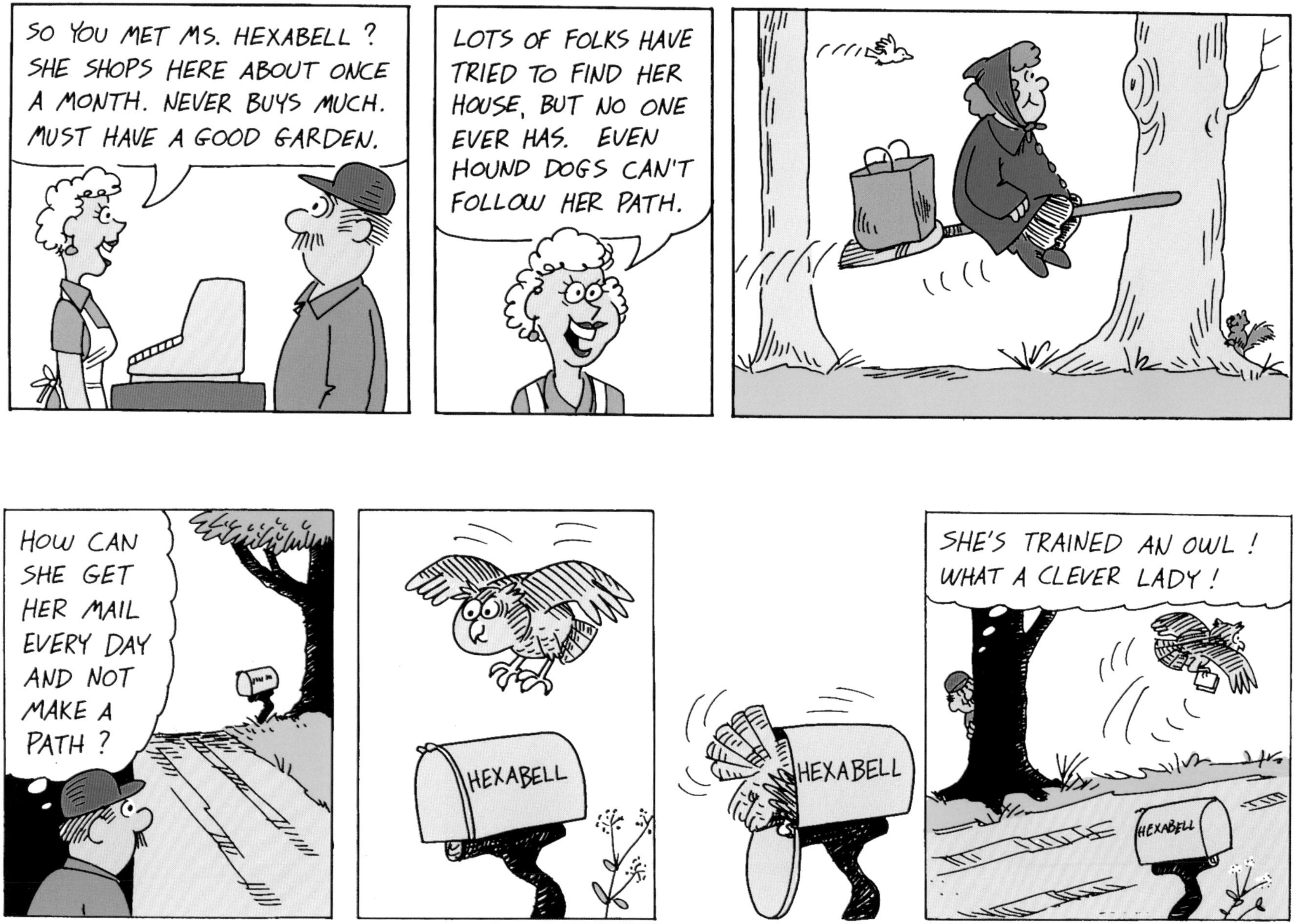
SO YOU MET MS. HEXABELL ? SHE SHOPS HERE ABOUT ONCE A MONTH. NEVER BUYS MUCH. MUST HAVE A GOOD GARDEN.
LOTS OF FOLKS HAVE TRIED TO FIND HER HOUSE, BUT NO ONE EVER HAS. EVEN HOUND DOGS CAN'T FOLLOW HER PATH.
HOW CAN SHE GET HER MAIL EVERY DAY AND NOT MAKE A PATH ?
HEXABELL
HEXABELL
SHE'S TRAINED AN OWL ! WHAT A CLEVER LADY !
HEXABELL

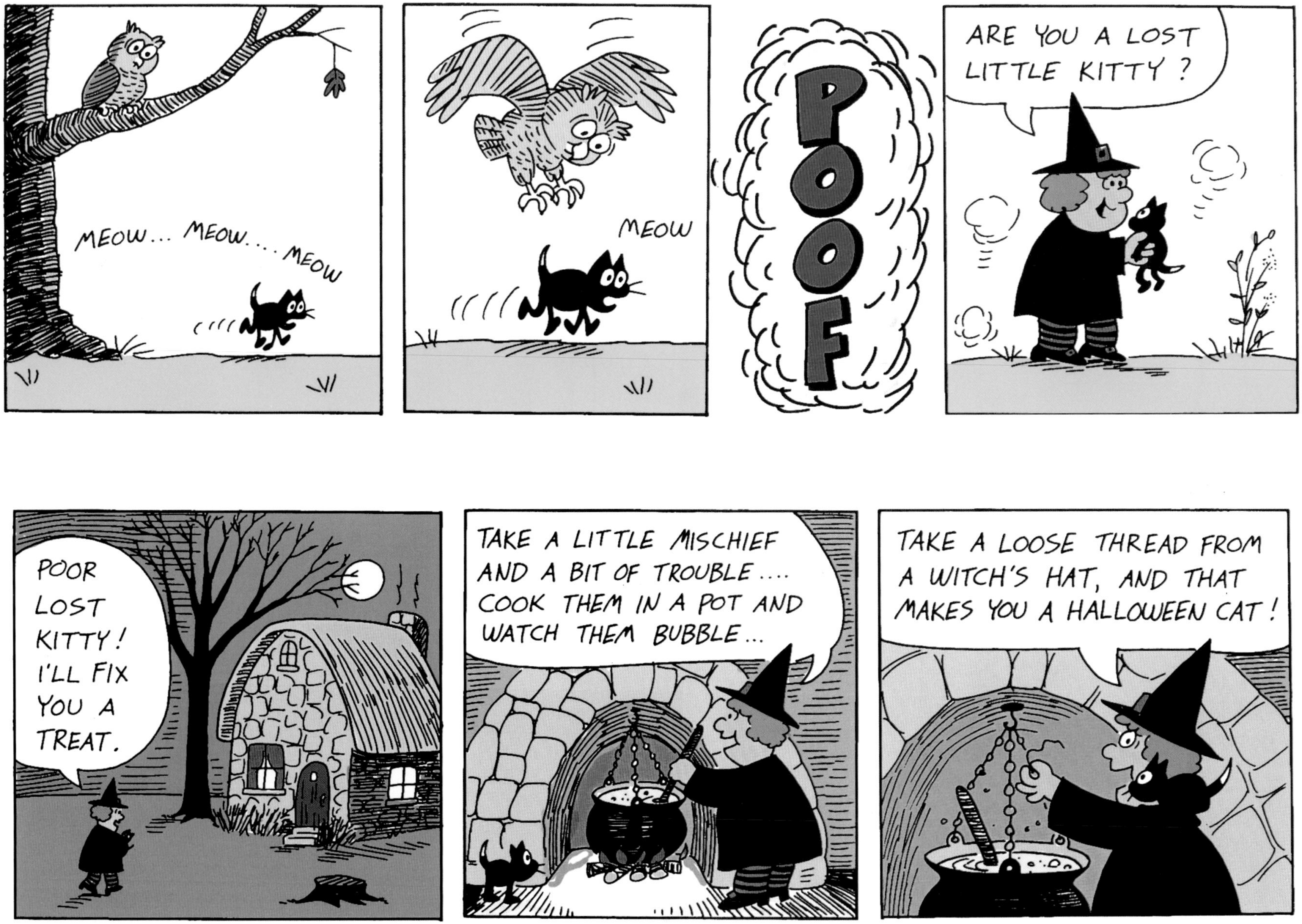
MEOW... MEOW.... MEOW
MEOW
POOF
ARE YOU A LOST LITTLE KITTY ?
POOR LOST KITTY! I'LL FIX YOU A TREAT.
TAKE A LITTLE MISCHIEF AND A BIT OF TROUBLE.... COOK THEM IN A POT AND WATCH THEM BUBBLE...
TAKE A LOOSE THREAD FROM A WITCH'S HAT, AND THAT MAKES YOU A HALLOWEEN CAT!

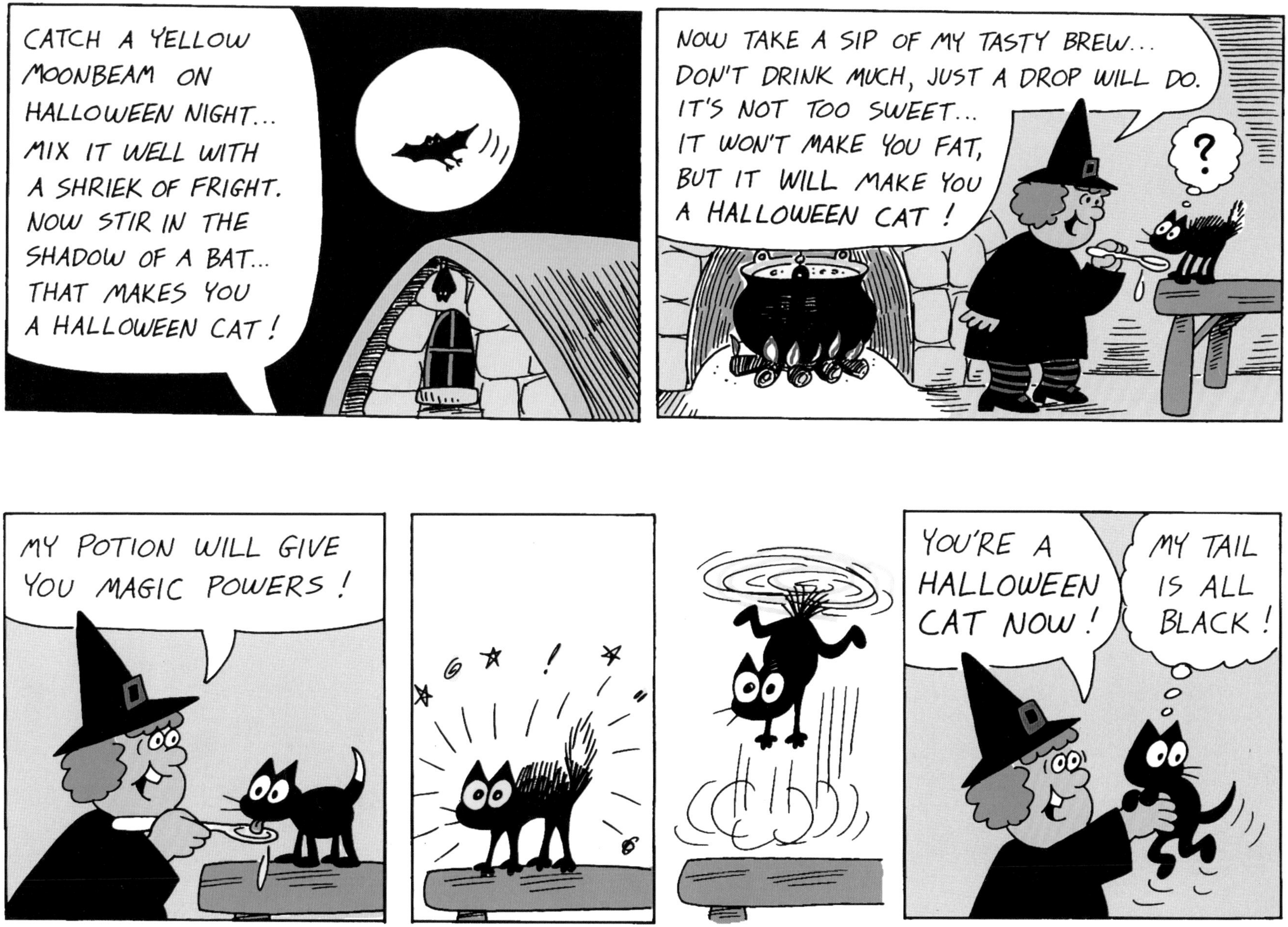
CATCH A YELLOW MOONBEAM ON HALLOWEEN NIGHT... MIX IT WELL WITH A SHRIEK OF FRIGHT. NOW STIR IN THE SHADOW OF A BAT... THAT MAKES YOU A HALLOWEEN CAT!
NOW TAKE A SIP OF MY TASTY BREW... DON'T DRINK MUCH, JUST A DROP WILL DO. IT'S NOT TOO SWEET... IT WON'T MAKE YOU FAT, BUT IT WILL MAKE YOU A HALLOWEEN CAT!
?
MY POTION WILL GIVE YOU MAGIC POWERS!
YOU'RE A HALLOWEEN CAT NOW!
MY TAIL IS ALL BLACK!

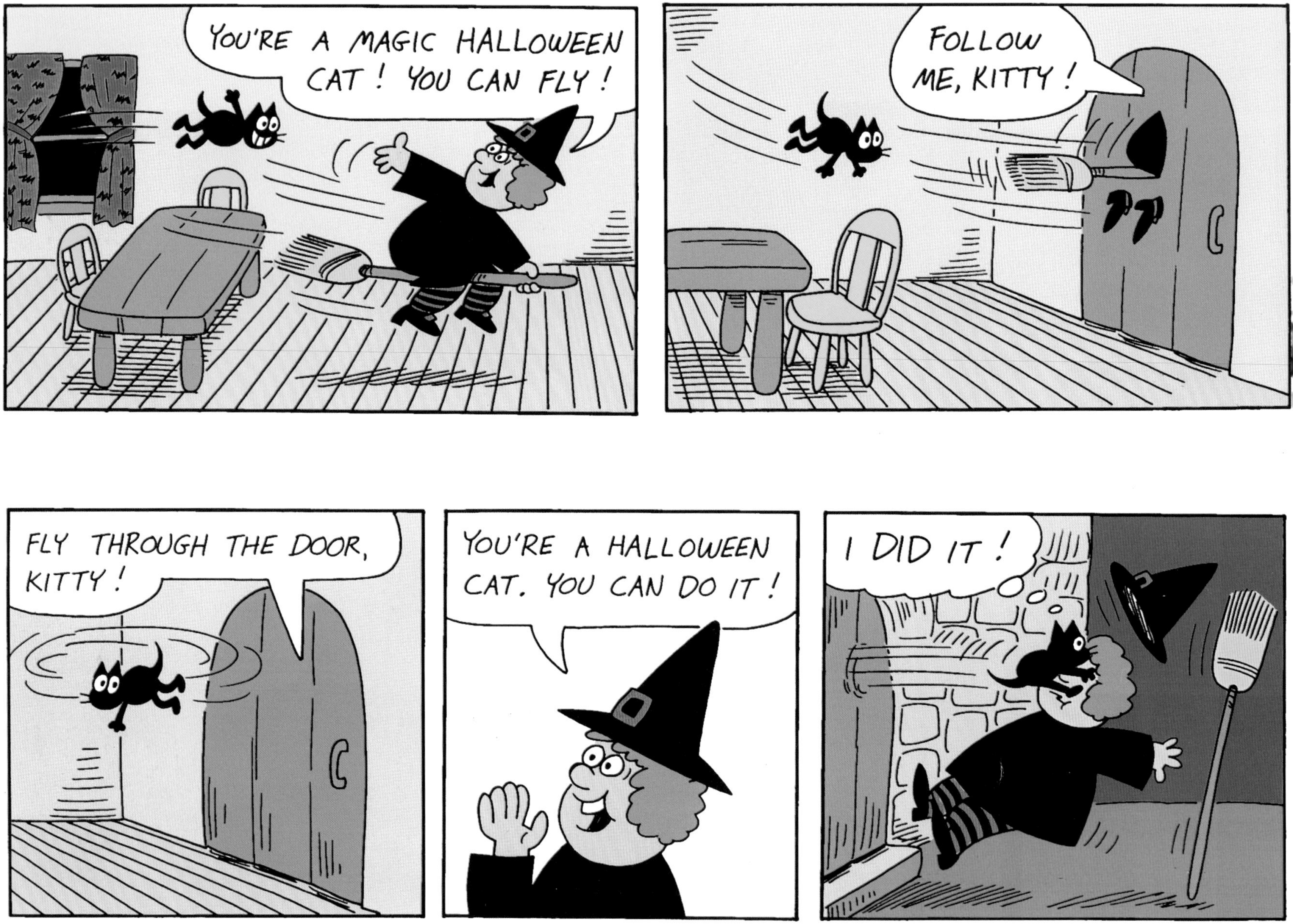
YOU'RE A MAGIC HALLOWEEN CAT! YOU CAN FLY!
FOLLOW ME, KITTY!
FLY THROUGH THE DOOR, KITTY!
YOU'RE A HALLOWEEN CAT. YOU CAN DO IT!
I DID IT!

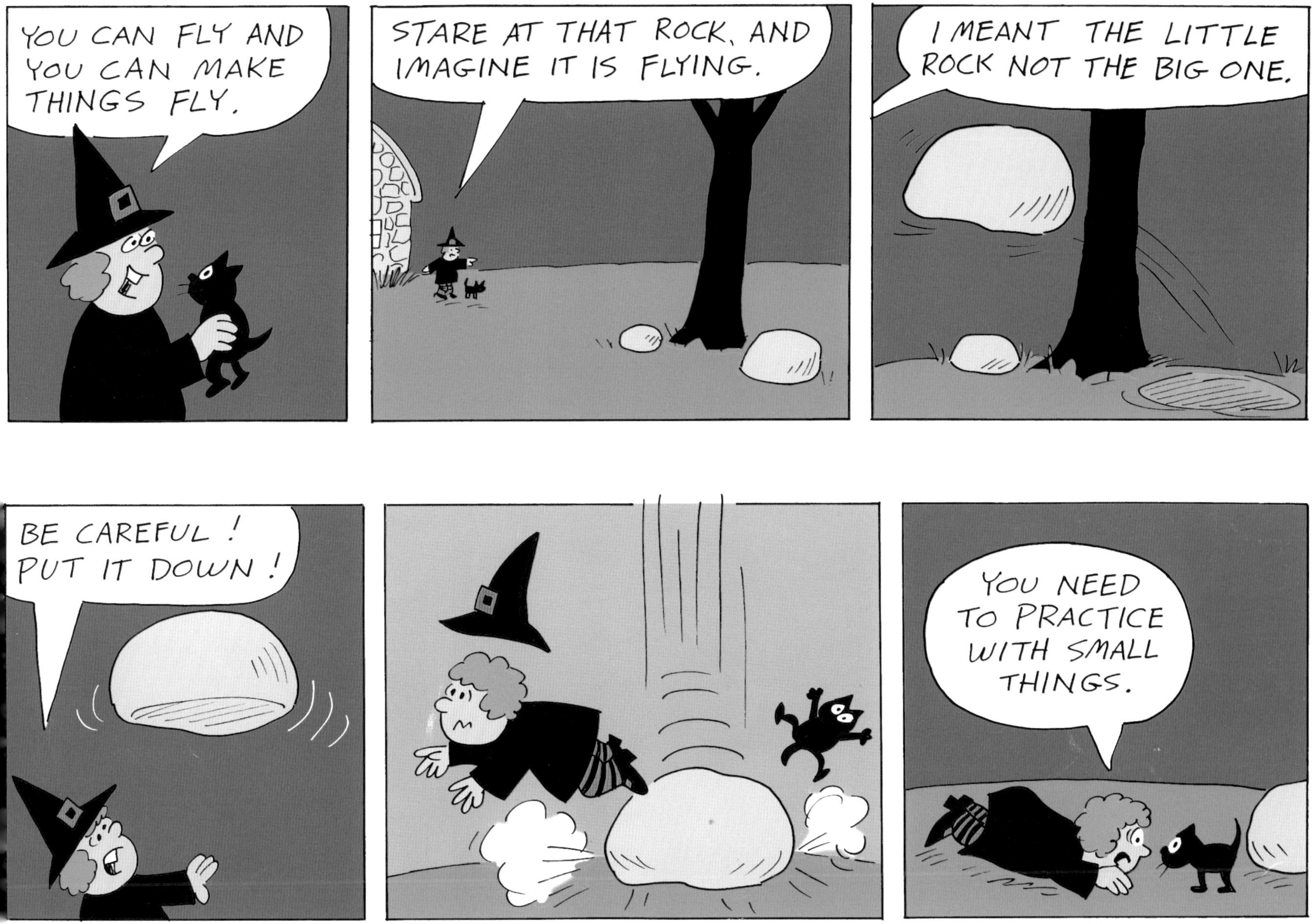
YOU CAN FLY AND YOU CAN MAKE THINGS FLY.
STARE AT THAT ROCK, AND IMAGINE IT IS FLYING.
I MEANT THE LITTLE ROCK NOT THE BIG ONE.
BE CAREFUL ! PUT IT DOWN !
YOU NEED TO PRACTICE WITH SMALL THINGS.

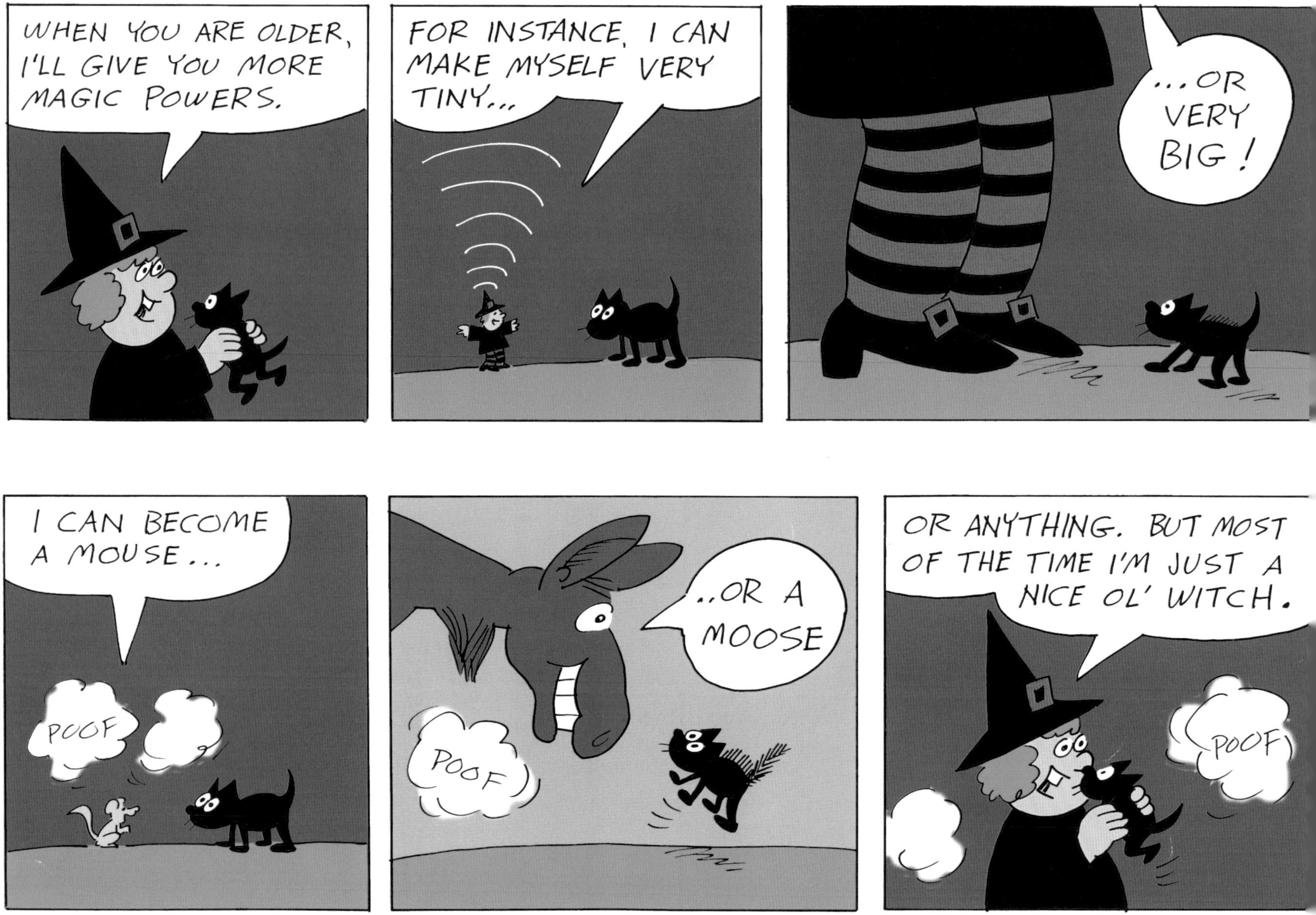
WHEN YOU ARE OLDER, I'LL GIVE YOU MORE MAGIC POWERS.
FOR INSTANCE, I CAN MAKE MYSELF VERY TINY...
...OR VERY BIG!
I CAN BECOME A MOUSE...
POOF
..OR A MOOSE
POOF
OR ANYTHING. BUT MOST OF THE TIME I'M JUST A NICE OL' WITCH.
POOF

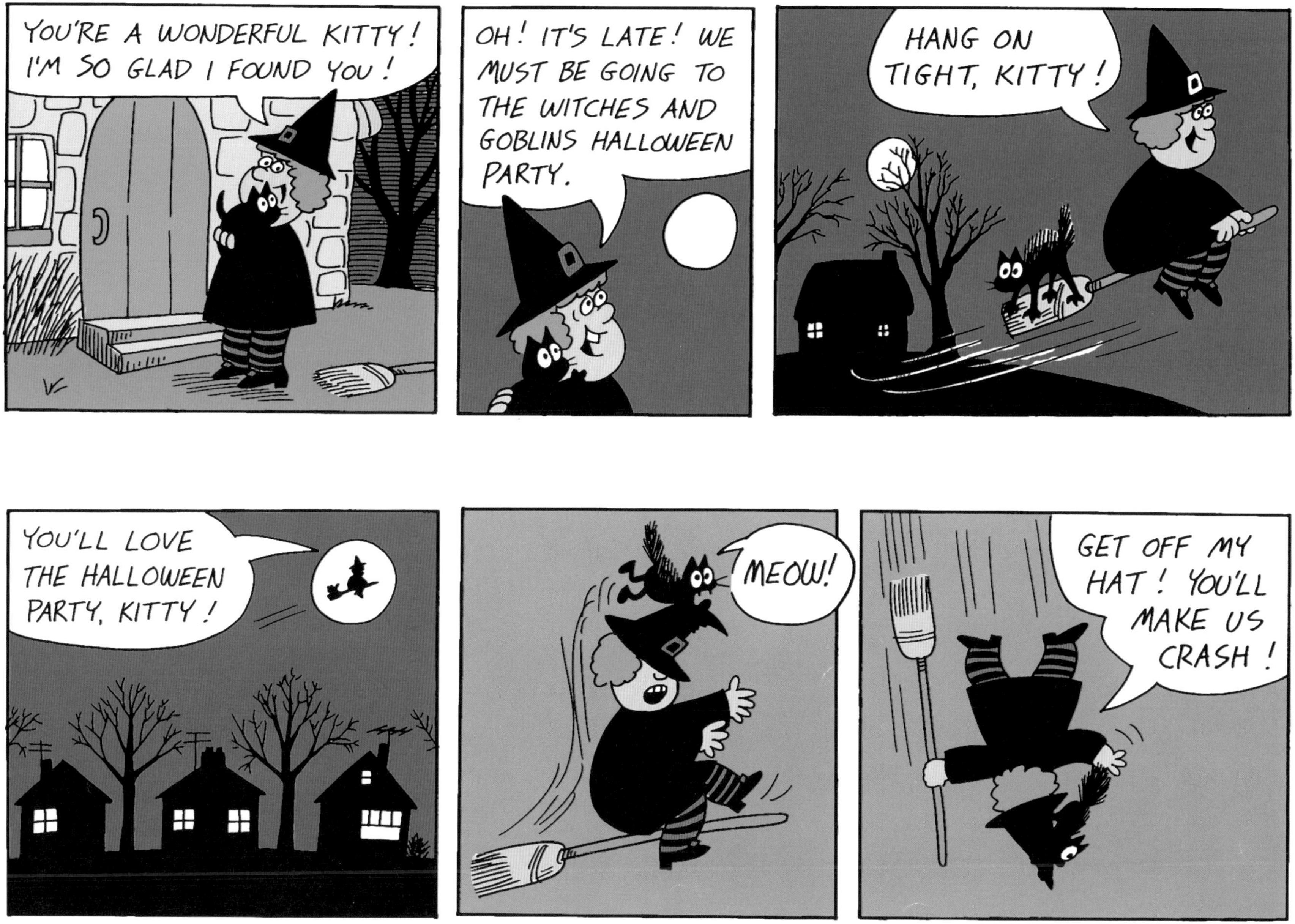
YOU'RE A WONDERFUL KITTY! I'M SO GLAD I FOUND YOU!
OH! IT'S LATE! WE MUST BE GOING TO THE WITCHES AND GOBLINS HALLOWEEN PARTY.
HANG ON TIGHT, KITTY!
YOU'LL LOVE THE HALLOWEEN PARTY, KITTY!
MEOW!
GET OFF MY HAT! YOU'LL MAKE US CRASH!

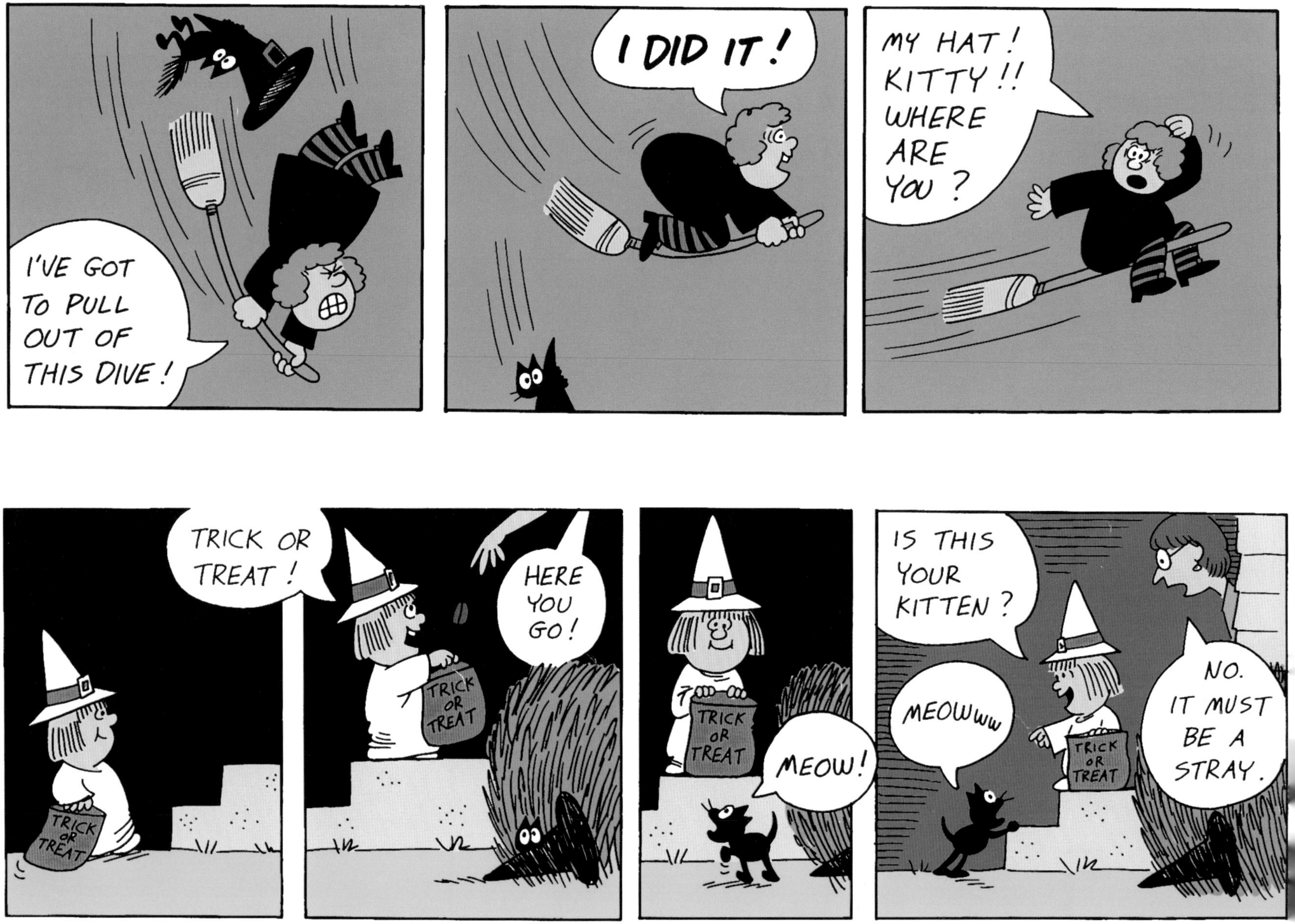
I'VE GOT TO PULL OUT OF THIS DIVE!
I DID IT!
MY HAT! KITTY!! WHERE ARE YOU?
TRICK OR TREAT
TRICK OR TREAT!
HERE YOU GO!
TRICK OR TREAT
TRICK OR TREAT
MEOW!
IS THIS YOUR KITTEN?
MEOWww
NO. IT MUST BE A STRAY.
TRICK OR TREAT

MRS. JONES GAVE ME A CANDY BAR AND A KITTEN!

PRRRR

TRICK OR TREAT

YOU SHOULDN'T TAKE THAT KITTEN! IT MIGHT LIVE IN ONE OF THESE HOUSES.

IF IT'S NOT LOST, IT WON'T FOLLOW US. DON'T LOOK BACK!

TRICK OR TREAT

LET THE KITTEN GO BACK TO HIS OWN HOME.

TRICK OR TREAT

HE WILL BE HAPPY THERE.

TRICK OR TREAT

UNCLE WALLY... THE KITTEN WAS FLYING!

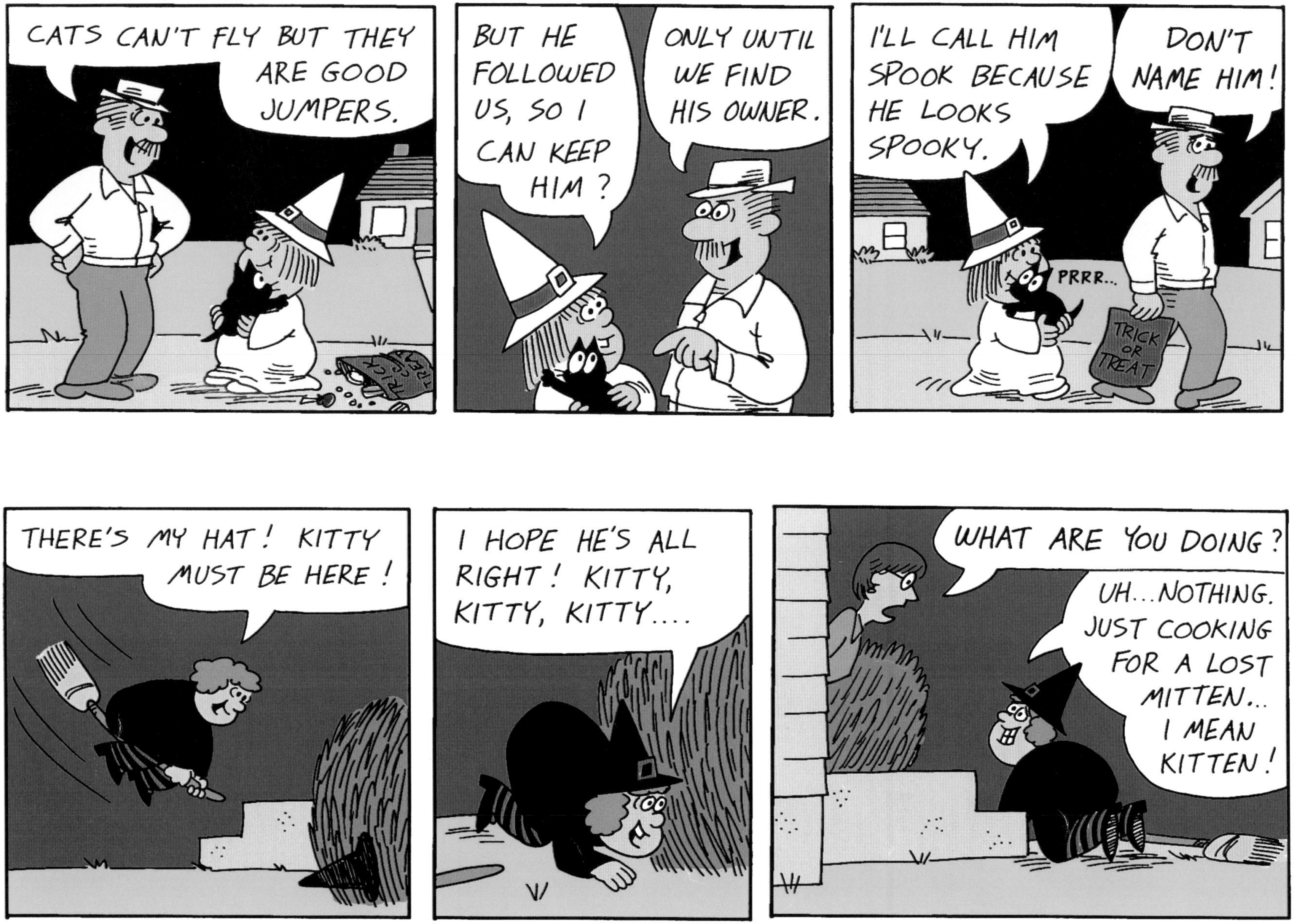
CATS CAN'T FLY BUT THEY ARE GOOD JUMPERS.
TRICK OR TREAT
BUT HE FOLLOWED US, SO I CAN KEEP HIM?
ONLY UNTIL WE FIND HIS OWNER.
I'LL CALL HIM SPOOK BECAUSE HE LOOKS SPOOKY.
DON'T NAME HIM!
PRRR...
TRICK OR TREAT
THERE'S MY HAT! KITTY MUST BE HERE!
I HOPE HE'S ALL RIGHT! KITTY, KITTY, KITTY....
WHAT ARE YOU DOING?
UH...NOTHING. JUST COOKING FOR A LOST MITTEN... I MEAN KITTEN!

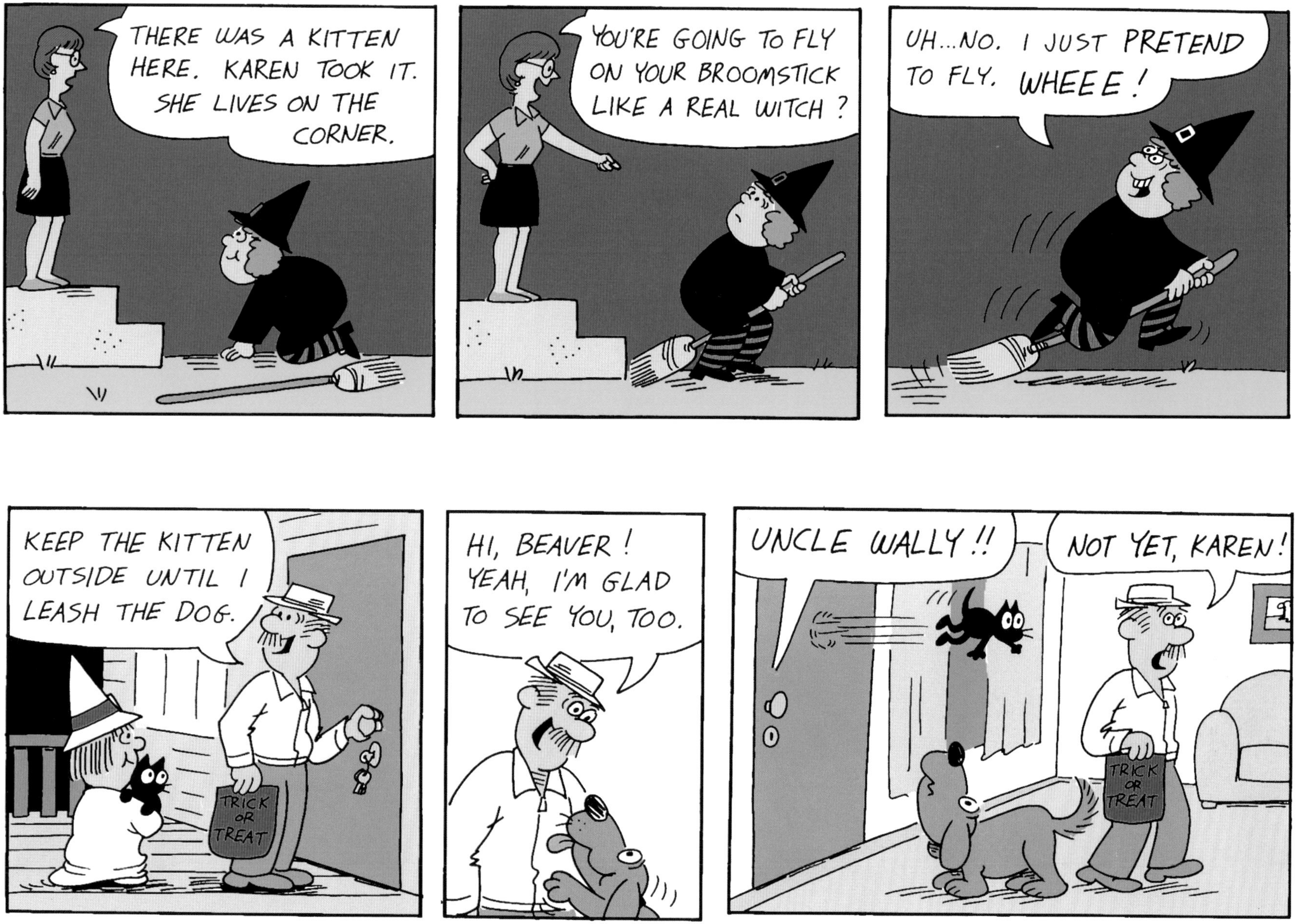
THERE WAS A KITTEN HERE. KAREN TOOK IT. SHE LIVES ON THE CORNER.
YOU'RE GOING TO FLY ON YOUR BROOMSTICK LIKE A REAL WITCH?
UH...NO. I JUST PRETEND TO FLY. WHEEE!
KEEP THE KITTEN OUTSIDE UNTIL I LEASH THE DOG.
TRICK OR TREAT
HI, BEAVER! YEAH, I'M GLAD TO SEE YOU, TOO.
UNCLE WALLY!!
NOT YET, KAREN!
TRICK OR TREAT

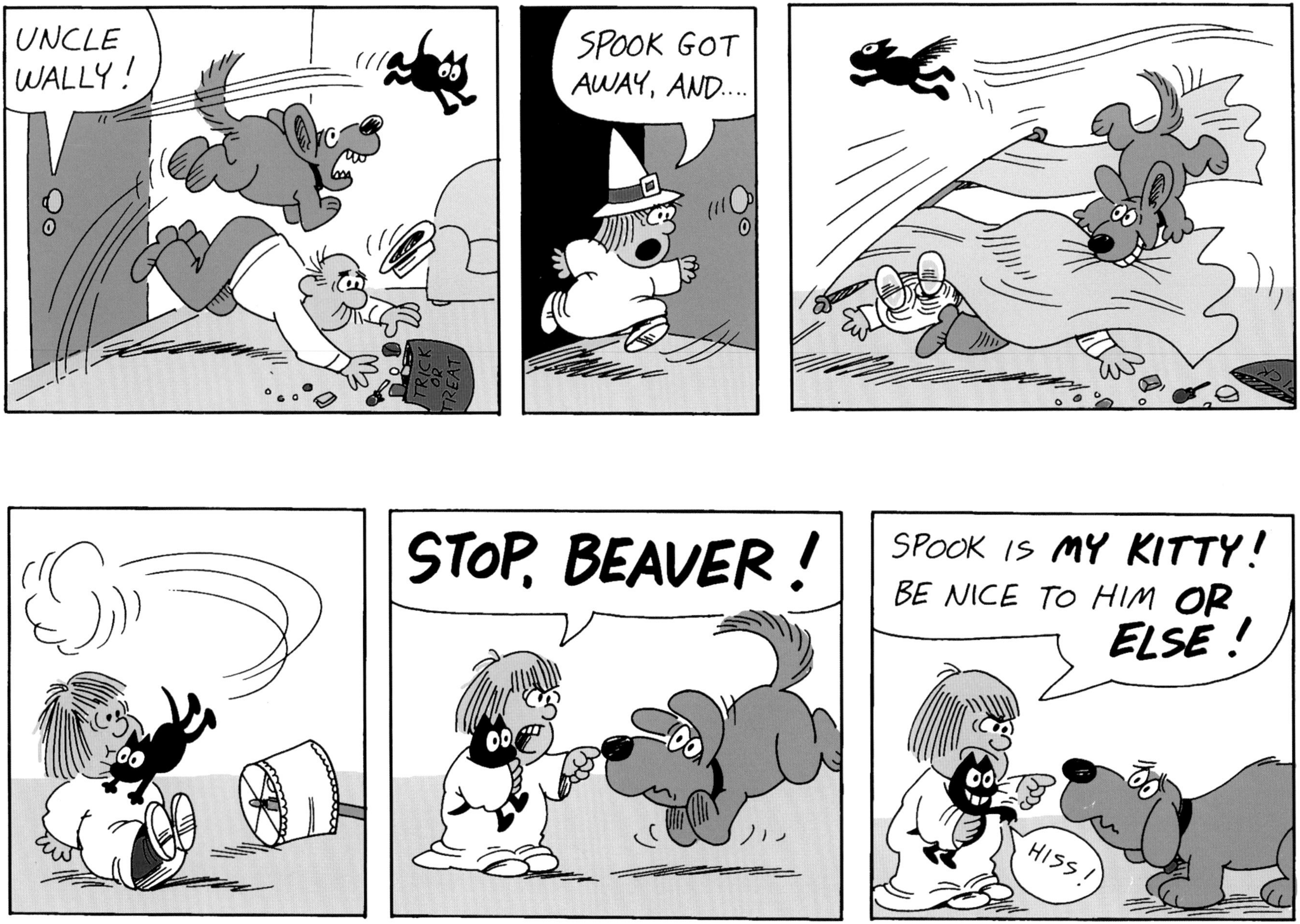
UNCLE WALLY!
TRICK OR TREAT
SPOOK GOT AWAY, AND....
STOP, BEAVER!
SPOOK IS MY KITTY! BE NICE TO HIM OR ELSE!
HISS!

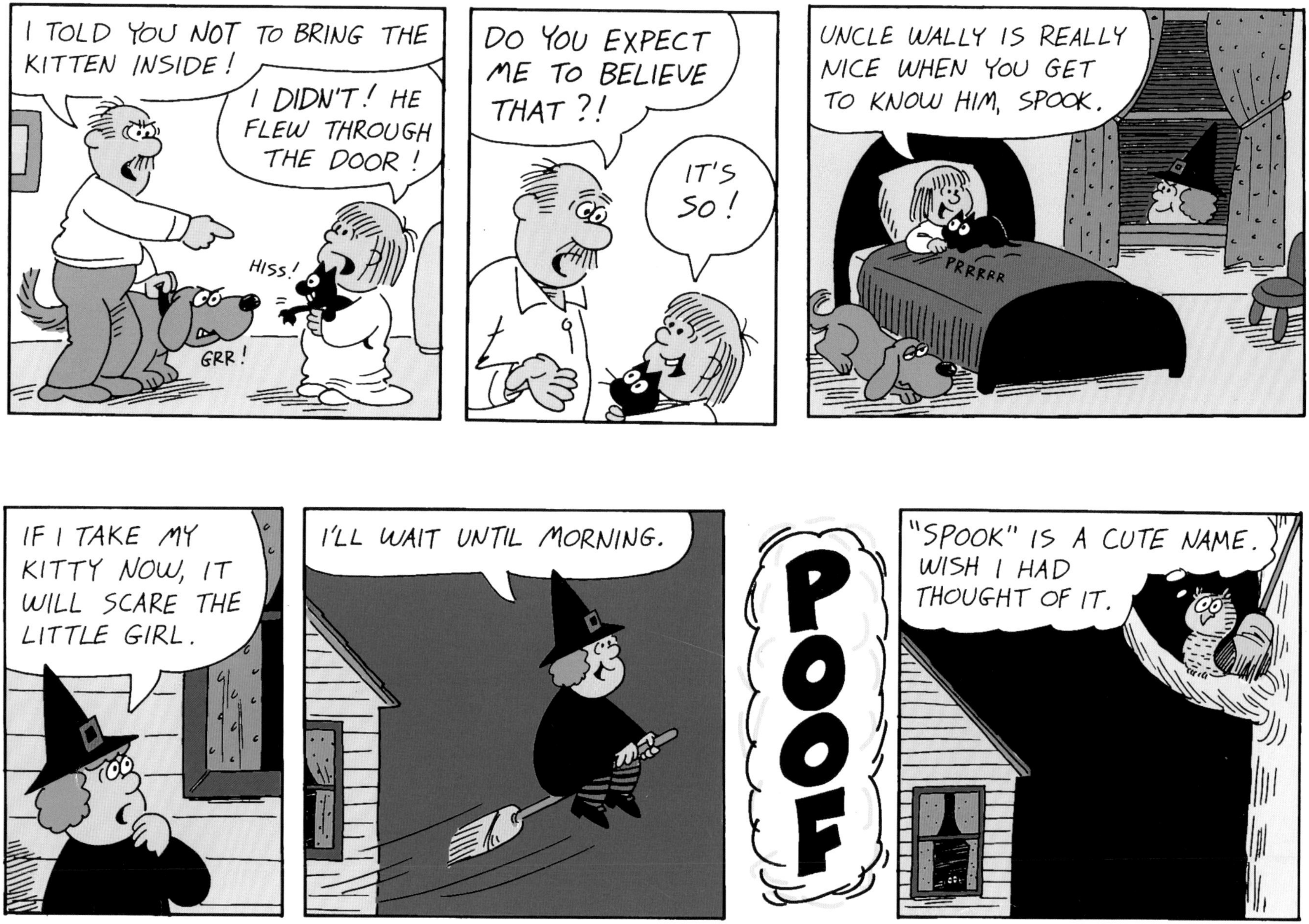
I TOLD YOU NOT TO BRING THE KITTEN INSIDE!
I DIDN'T! HE FLEW THROUGH THE DOOR!
HISS!
GRR!
DO YOU EXPECT ME TO BELIEVE THAT?!
IT'S SO!
UNCLE WALLY IS REALLY NICE WHEN YOU GET TO KNOW HIM, SPOOK.
PRRRRR
IF I TAKE MY KITTY NOW, IT WILL SCARE THE LITTLE GIRL.
I'LL WAIT UNTIL MORNING.
POOF
"SPOOK" IS A CUTE NAME. WISH I HAD THOUGHT OF IT.

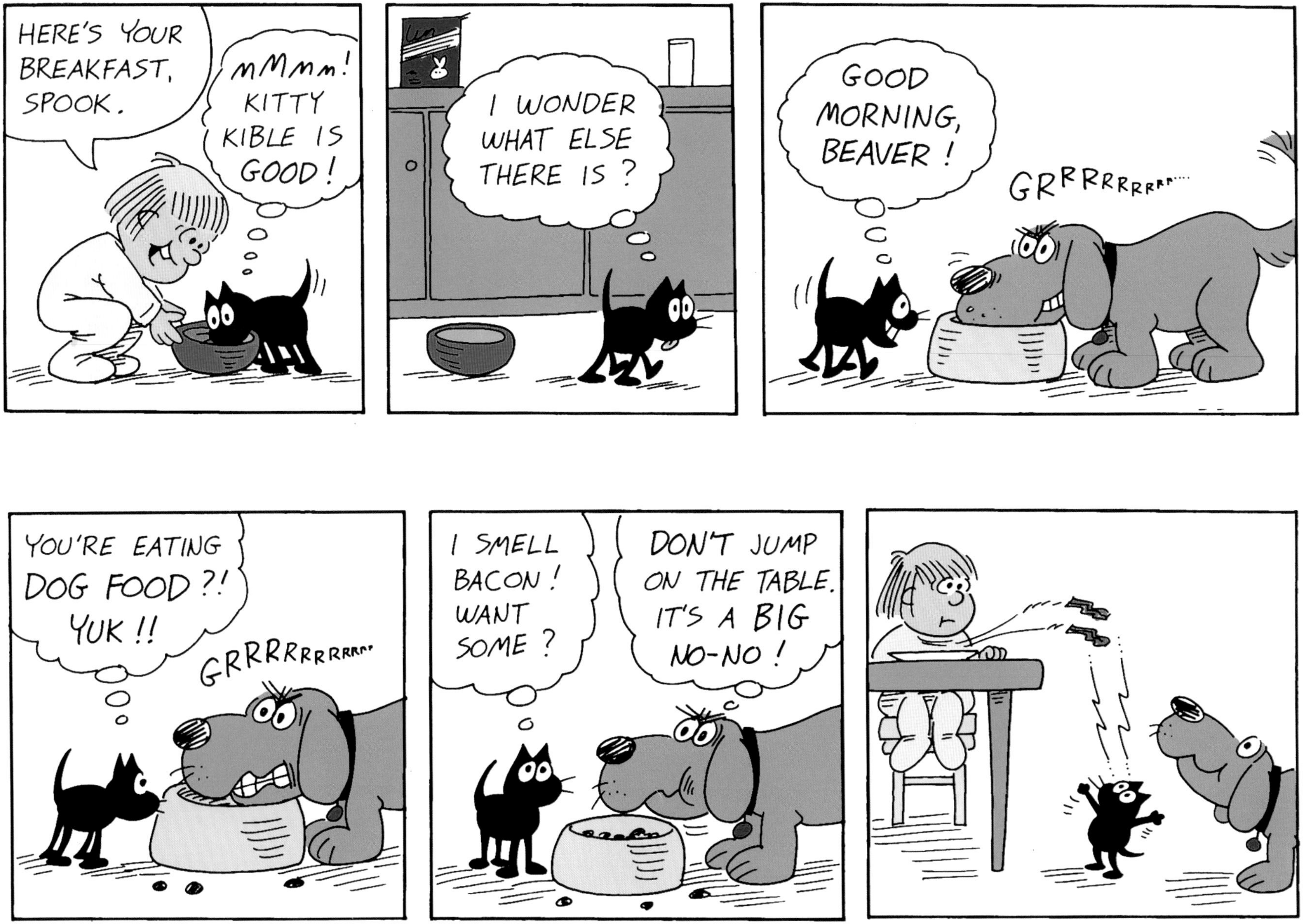
HERE'S YOUR BREAKFAST, SPOOK.
MMMMM! KITTY KIBLE IS GOOD!
I WONDER WHAT ELSE THERE IS ?
GOOD MORNING, BEAVER !
GRRRRRRRRR....
YOU'RE EATING DOG FOOD ?! YUK !!
GRRRRRRRRRR
I SMELL BACON ! WANT SOME ?
DON'T JUMP ON THE TABLE. IT'S A BIG NO-NO !

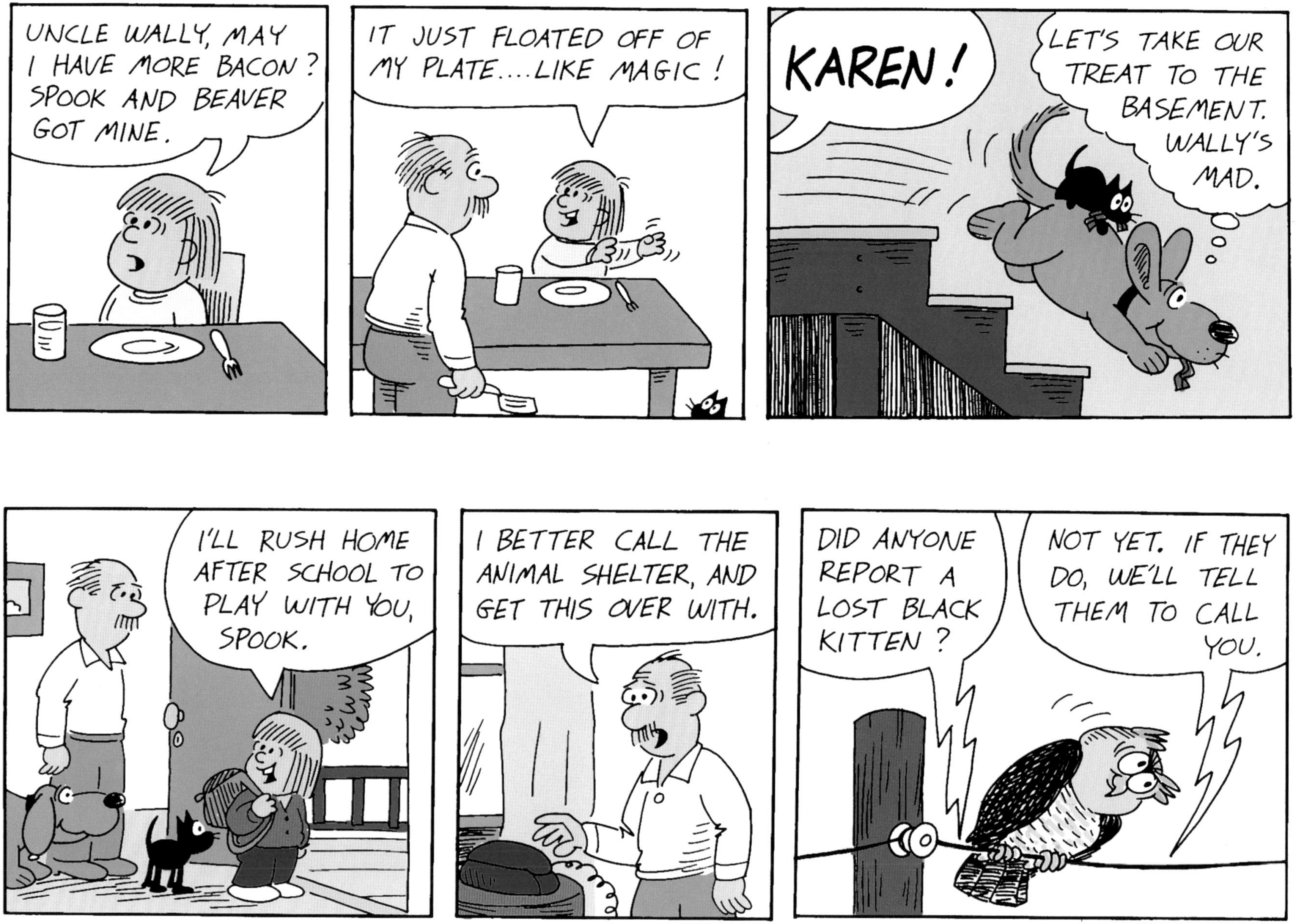
UNCLE WALLY, MAY I HAVE MORE BACON? SPOOK AND BEAVER GOT MINE.
IT JUST FLOATED OFF OF MY PLATE....LIKE MAGIC!
KAREN!
LET'S TAKE OUR TREAT TO THE BASEMENT. WALLY'S MAD.
I'LL RUSH HOME AFTER SCHOOL TO PLAY WITH YOU, SPOOK.
I BETTER CALL THE ANIMAL SHELTER, AND GET THIS OVER WITH.
DID ANYONE REPORT A LOST BLACK KITTEN?
NOT YET. IF THEY DO, WE'LL TELL THEM TO CALL YOU.

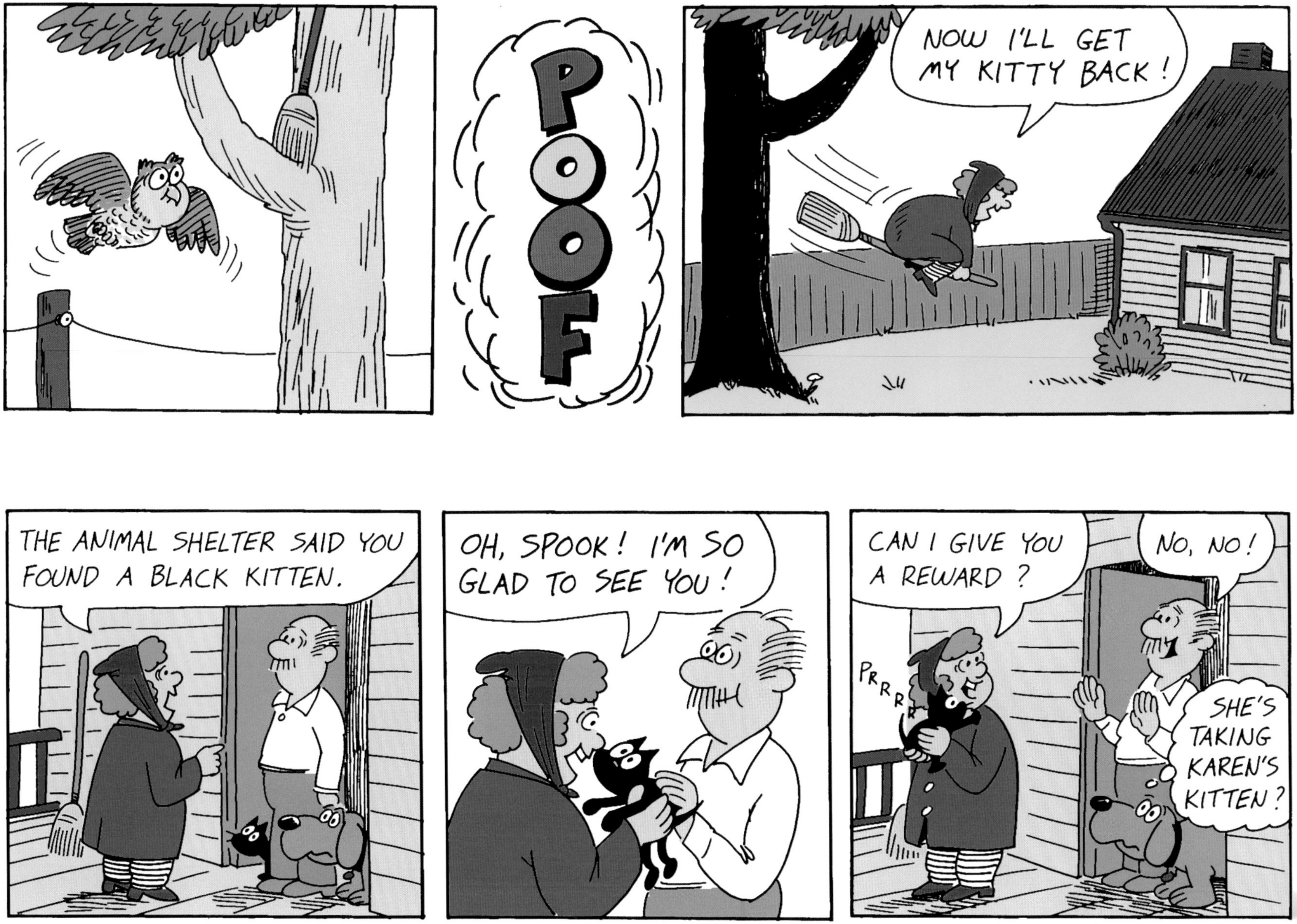
POOF
NOW I'LL GET MY KITTY BACK!
THE ANIMAL SHELTER SAID YOU FOUND A BLACK KITTEN.
OH, SPOOK! I'M SO GLAD TO SEE YOU!
CAN I GIVE YOU A REWARD?
NO, NO!
PRRRR
SHE'S TAKING KAREN'S KITTEN?

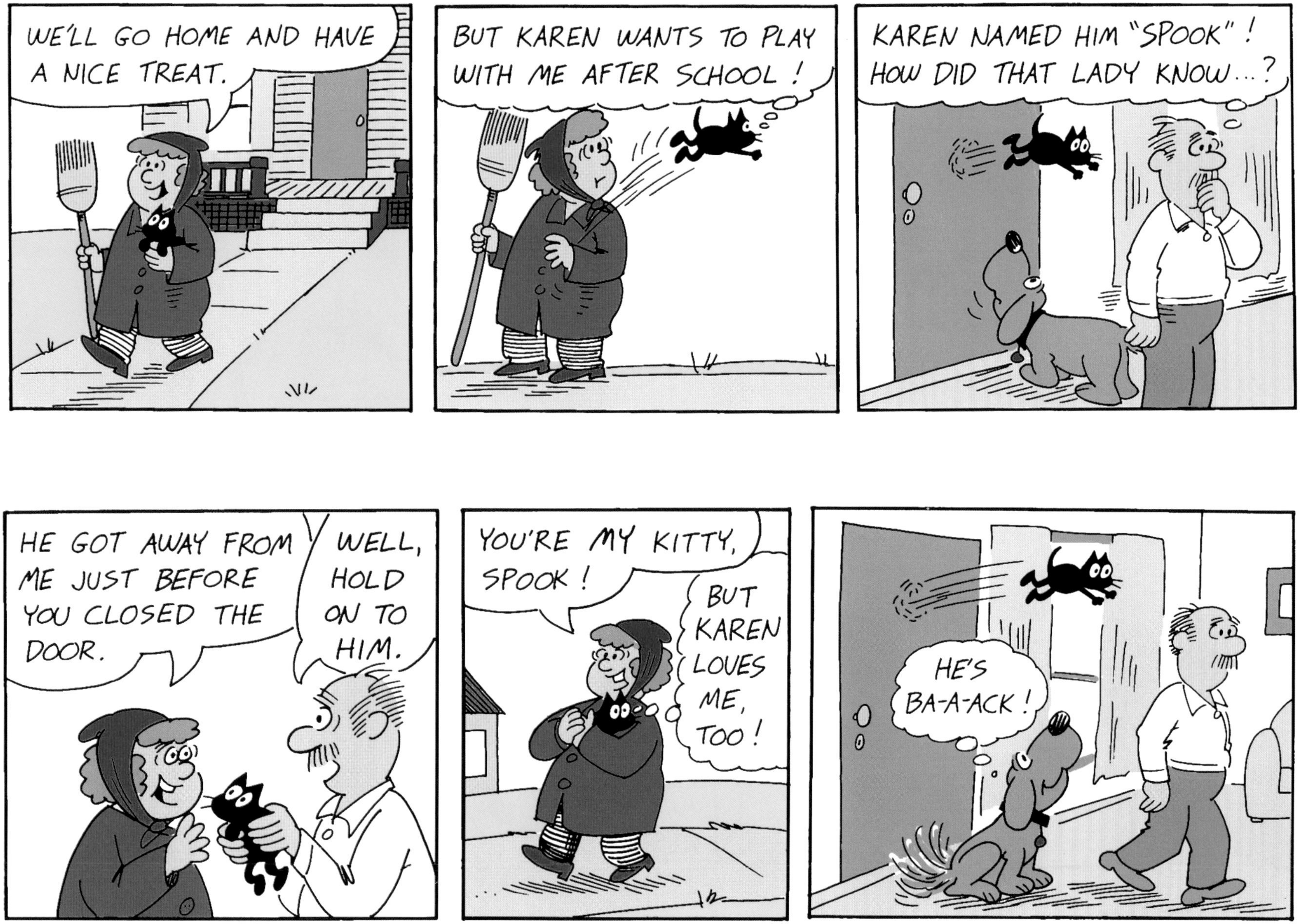
WE'LL GO HOME AND HAVE A NICE TREAT.
BUT KAREN WANTS TO PLAY WITH ME AFTER SCHOOL!
KAREN NAMED HIM "SPOOK"! HOW DID THAT LADY KNOW...?
HE GOT AWAY FROM ME JUST BEFORE YOU CLOSED THE DOOR.
WELL, HOLD ON TO HIM.
YOU'RE MY KITTY, SPOOK!
BUT KAREN LOVES ME, TOO!
HE'S BA-A-ACK!

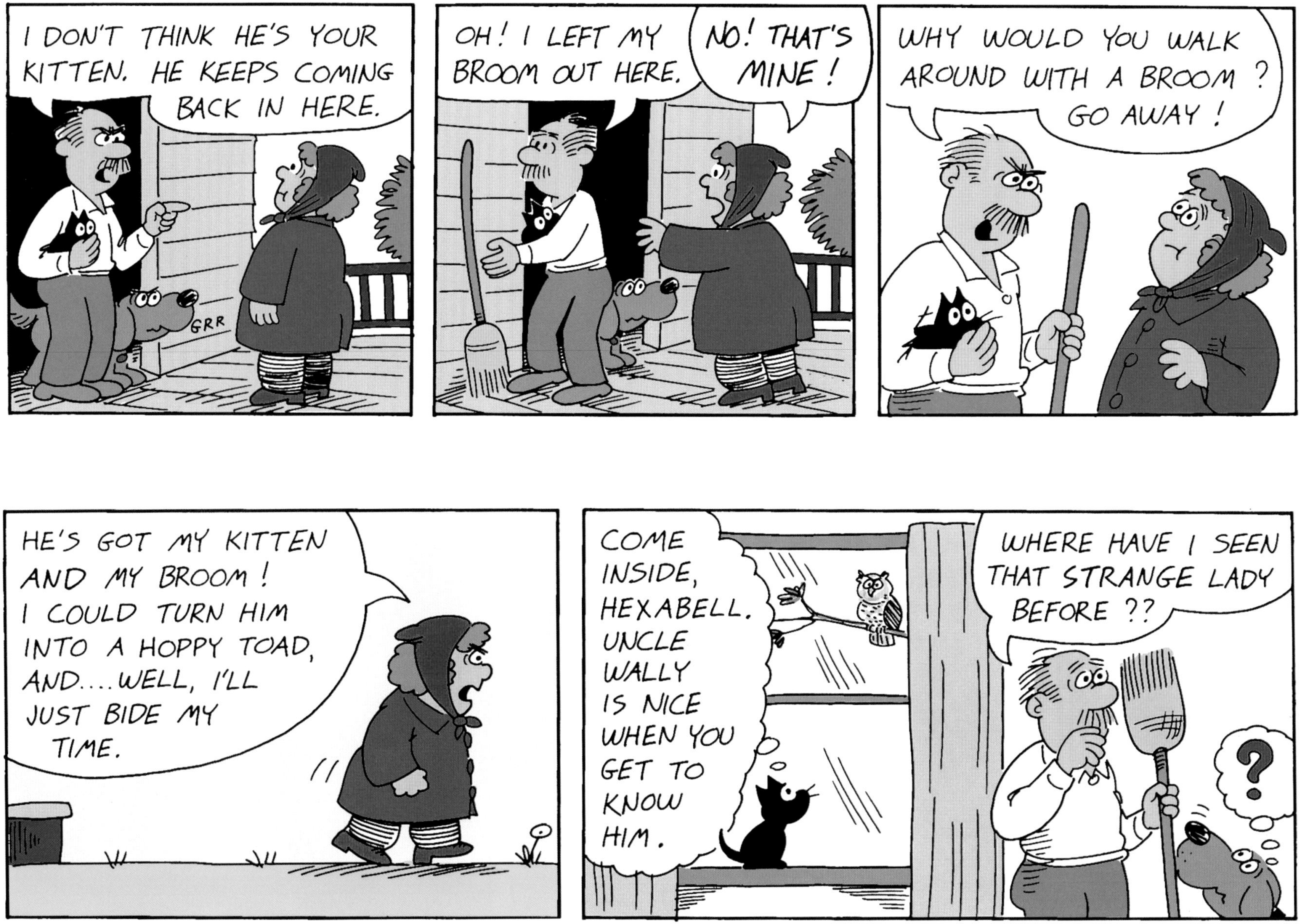
I DON'T THINK HE'S YOUR KITTEN. HE KEEPS COMING BACK IN HERE.
GRR
OH! I LEFT MY BROOM OUT HERE.
NO! THAT'S MINE!
WHY WOULD YOU WALK AROUND WITH A BROOM? GO AWAY!
HE'S GOT MY KITTEN AND MY BROOM! I COULD TURN HIM INTO A HOPPY TOAD, AND....WELL, I'LL JUST BIDE MY TIME.
COME INSIDE, HEXABELL. UNCLE WALLY IS NICE WHEN YOU GET TO KNOW HIM.
WHERE HAVE I SEEN THAT STRANGE LADY BEFORE??
?

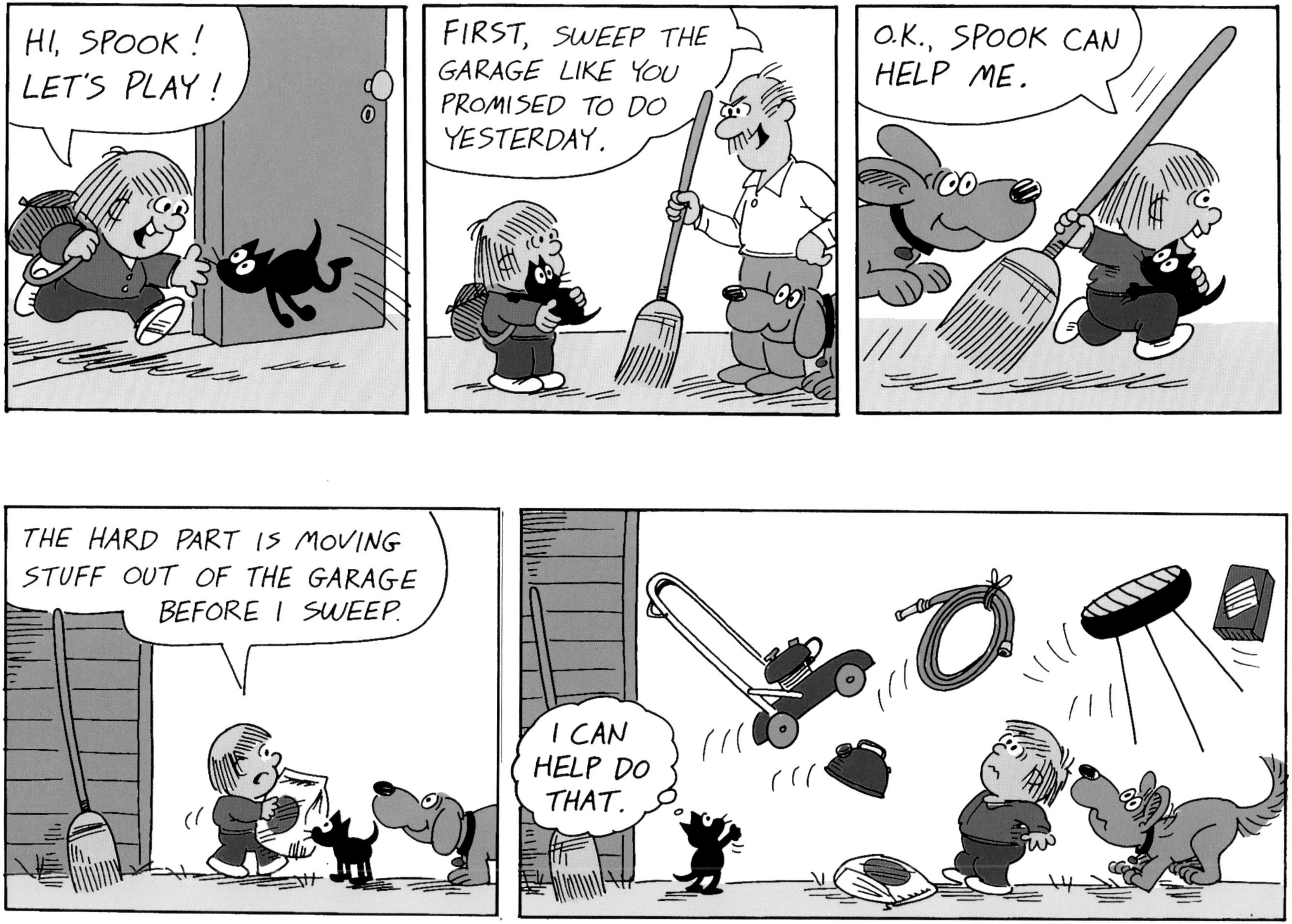
HI, SPOOK!
LET'S PLAY!
FIRST, SWEEP THE GARAGE LIKE YOU PROMISED TO DO YESTERDAY.
O.K., SPOOK CAN HELP ME.
THE HARD PART IS MOVING STUFF OUT OF THE GARAGE BEFORE I SWEEP.
I CAN HELP DO THAT.

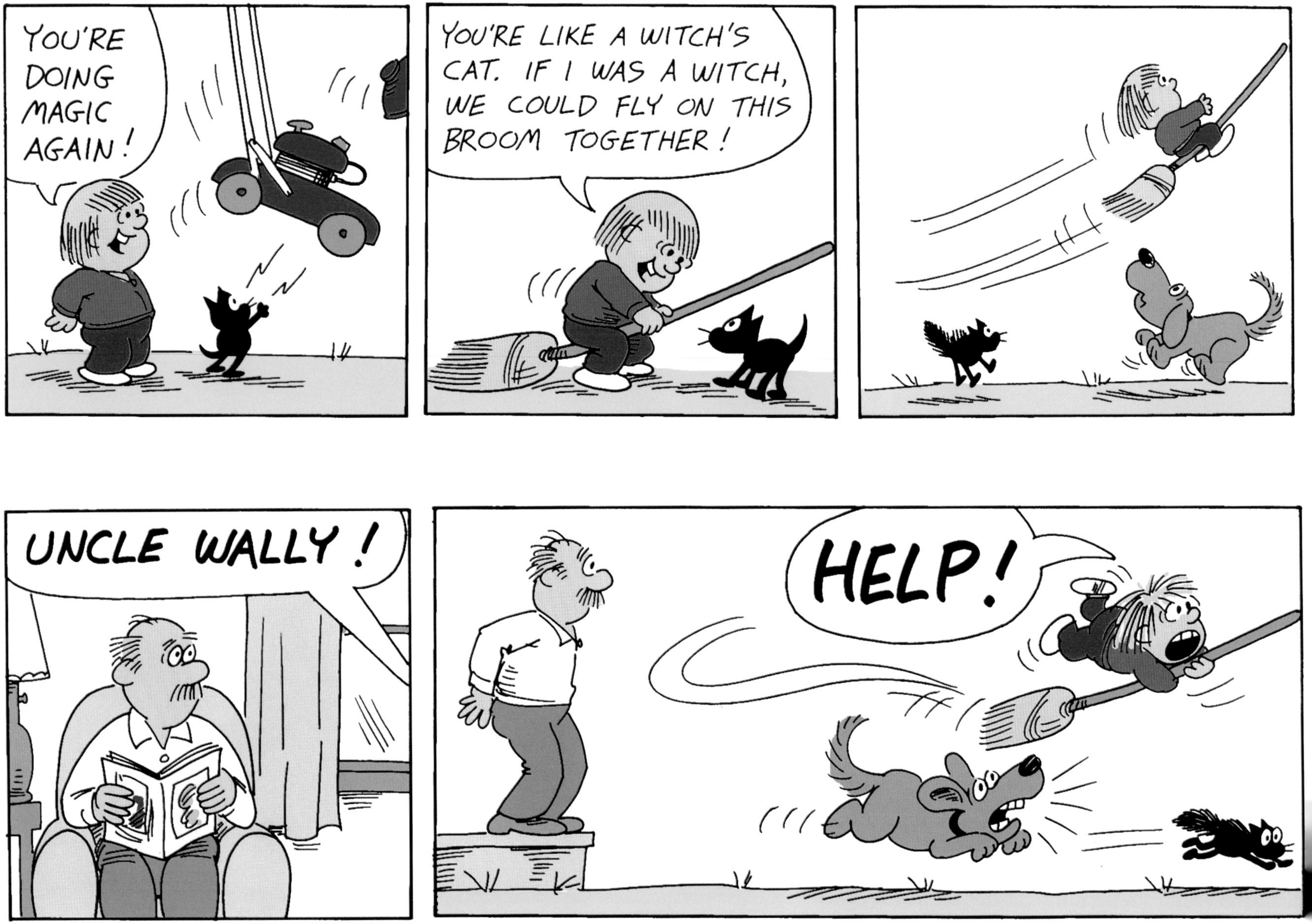
YOU'RE DOING MAGIC AGAIN!
YOU'RE LIKE A WITCH'S CAT. IF I WAS A WITCH, WE COULD FLY ON THIS BROOM TOGETHER!
UNCLE WALLY!
HELP!

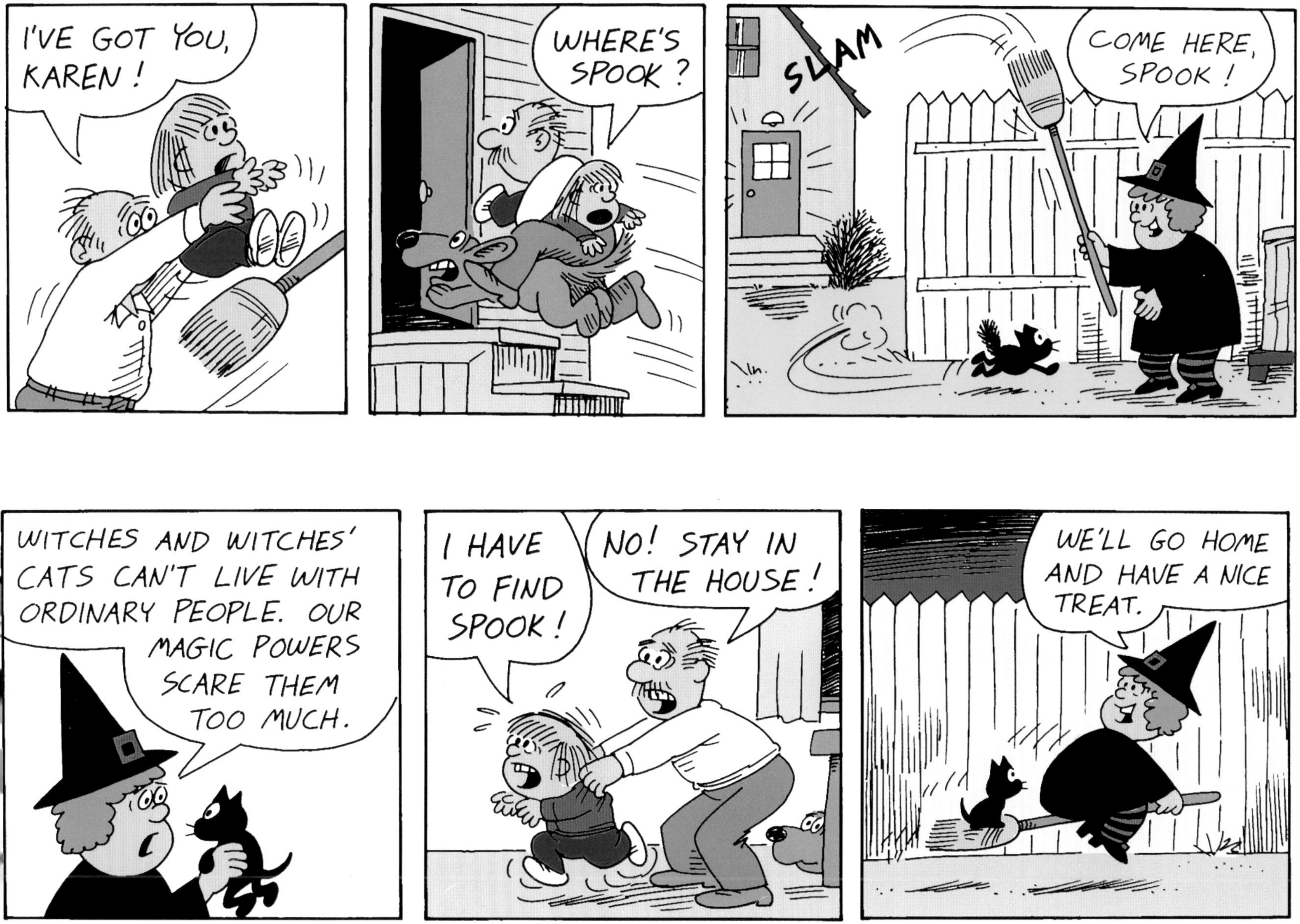
I'VE GOT YOU, KAREN!
WHERE'S SPOOK?
SLAM
COME HERE, SPOOK!
WITCHES AND WITCHES' CATS CAN'T LIVE WITH ORDINARY PEOPLE. OUR MAGIC POWERS SCARE THEM TOO MUCH.
I HAVE TO FIND SPOOK!
NO! STAY IN THE HOUSE!
WE'LL GO HOME AND HAVE A NICE TREAT.

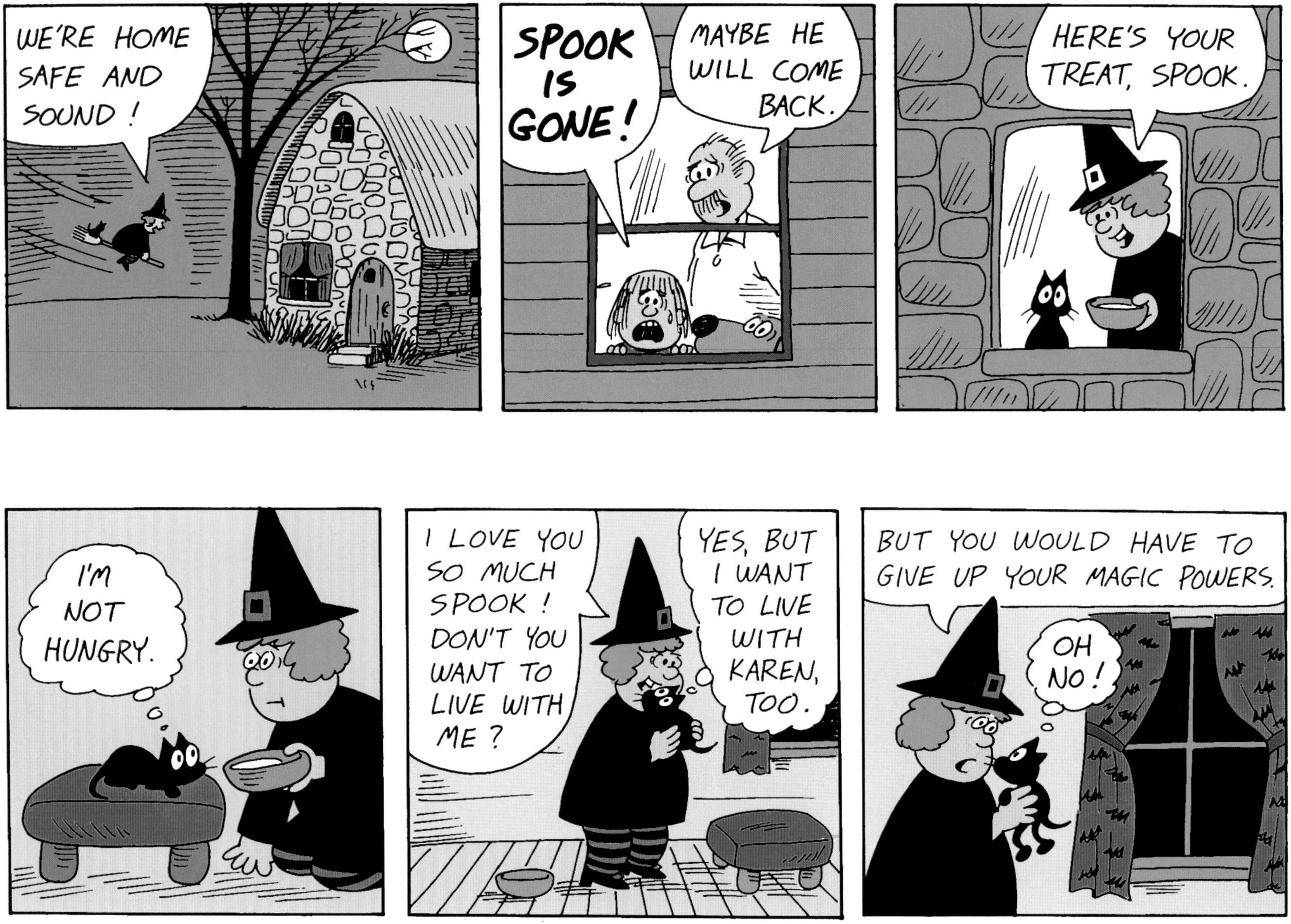

WE'RE HOME SAFE AND SOUND!
SPOOK IS GONE!
MAYBE HE WILL COME BACK.
HERE'S YOUR TREAT, SPOOK.
I'M NOT HUNGRY.
I LOVE YOU SO MUCH SPOOK! DON'T YOU WANT TO LIVE WITH ME?
YES, BUT I WANT TO LIVE WITH KAREN, TOO.
BUT YOU WOULD HAVE TO GIVE UP YOUR MAGIC POWERS.
OH NO!

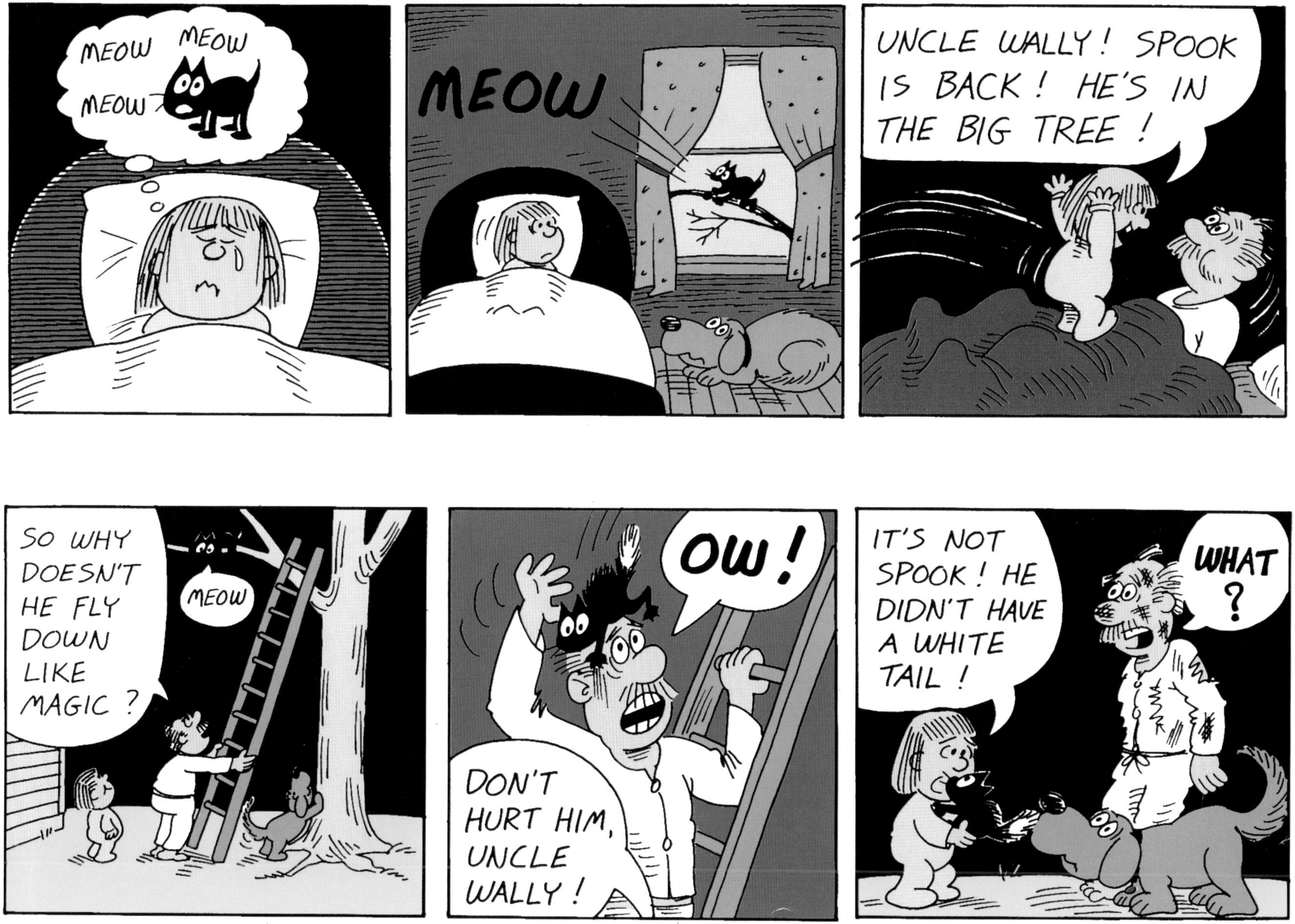
MEOW MEOW
MEOW
MEOW
UNCLE WALLY! SPOOK IS BACK! HE'S IN THE BIG TREE!
SO WHY DOESN'T HE FLY DOWN LIKE MAGIC?
MEOW
OW!
DON'T HURT HIM, UNCLE WALLY!
IT'S NOT SPOOK! HE DIDN'T HAVE A WHITE TAIL!
WHAT?

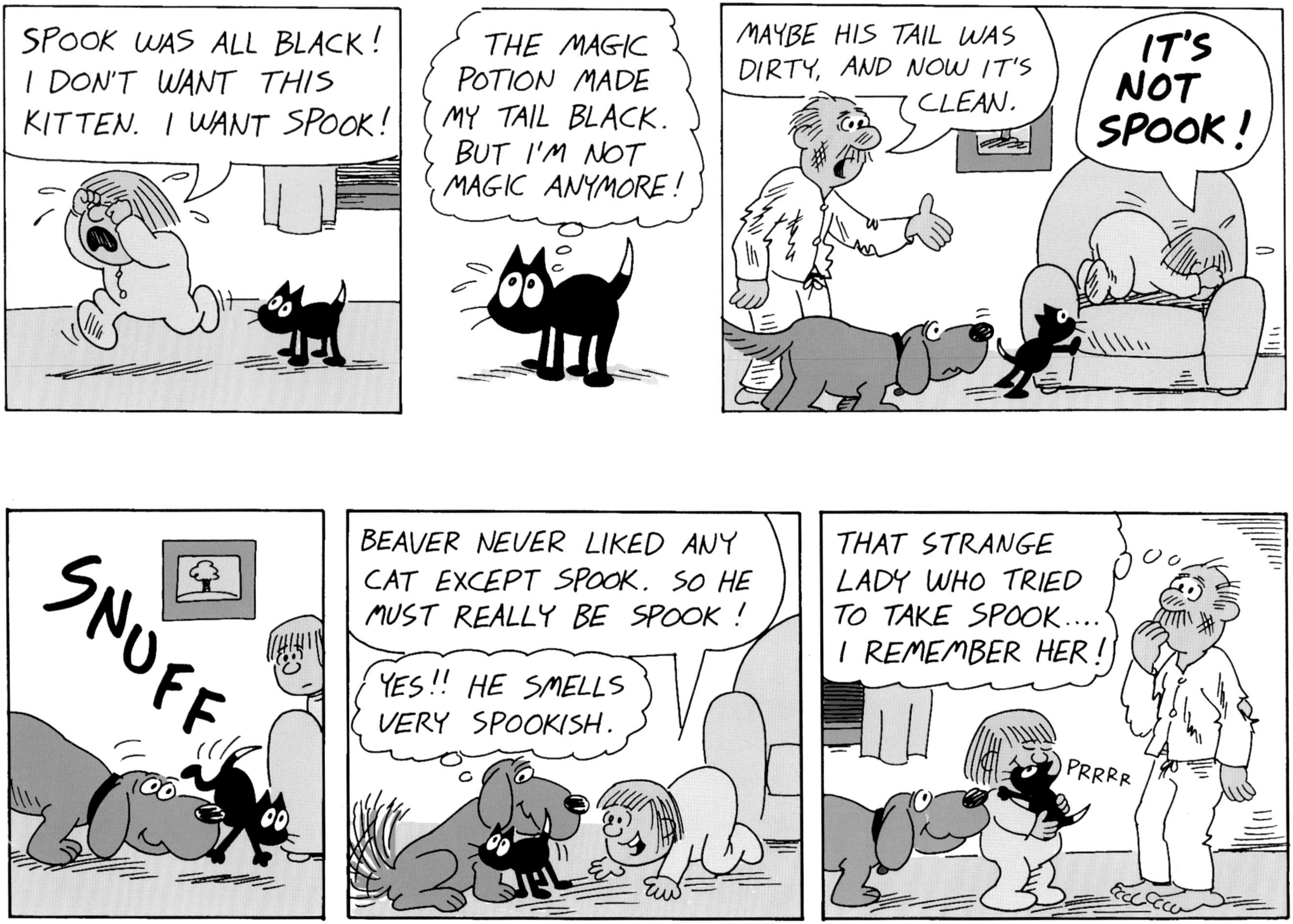
SPOOK WAS ALL BLACK! I DON'T WANT THIS KITTEN. I WANT SPOOK!
THE MAGIC POTION MADE MY TAIL BLACK. BUT I'M NOT MAGIC ANYMORE!
MAYBE HIS TAIL WAS DIRTY, AND NOW IT'S CLEAN.
IT'S NOT SPOOK!
SNUFF
BEAVER NEVER LIKED ANY CAT EXCEPT SPOOK. SO HE MUST REALLY BE SPOOK!
YES!! HE SMELLS VERY SPOOKISH.
THAT STRANGE LADY WHO TRIED TO TAKE SPOOK.... I REMEMBER HER!
PRRRRR

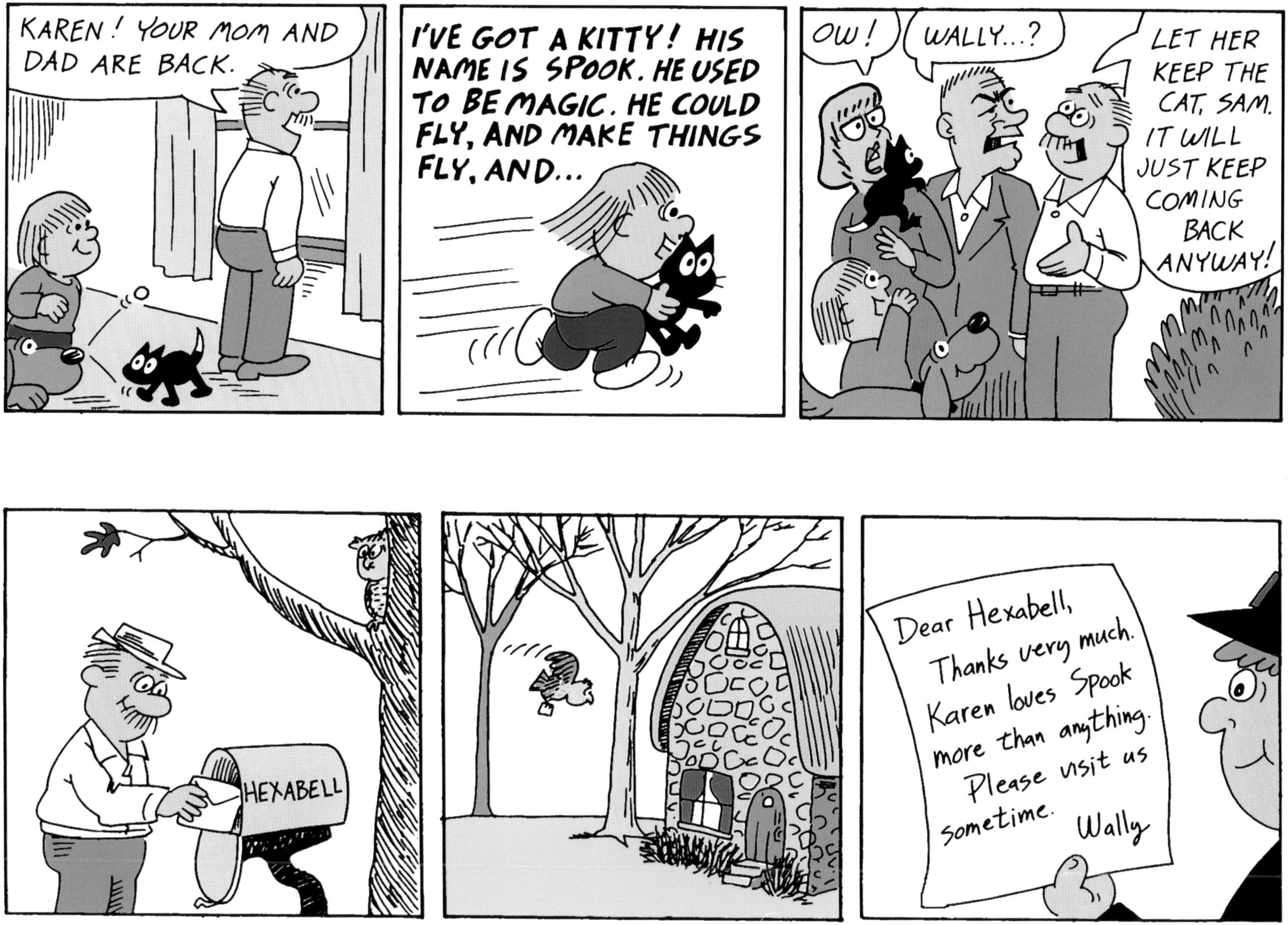
KAREN! YOUR MOM AND DAD ARE BACK.
I'VE GOT A KITTY! HIS NAME IS SPOOK. HE USED TO BE MAGIC. HE COULD FLY, AND MAKE THINGS FLY, AND...
OW!
WALLY...?
LET HER KEEP THE CAT, SAM. IT WILL JUST KEEP COMING BACK ANYWAY!
HEXABELL
Dear Hexabell,
Thanks very much.
Karen loves Spook
more than anything.
Please visit us
sometime.
Wally

THAT MAKES YOU A HALLOWEEN CAT

1. Take a little mischief   and a bit of trouble.   Cook them in a pot and watch them bubble.

2. Catch a yellow moonbeam on Halloween night.   And mix it well with a shriek of fright.

1. Take a loose thread   from a witch's hat.   That makes you a Halloween cat.

2. Now stir in   the shadow of a bat.   That makes you a Halloween cat.

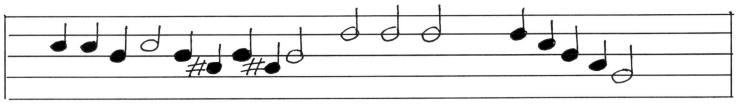

3. Now take a sip   of my tasty brew.   Don't drink much   just a drop will do.

3. It's not too sweet. It won't make you fat.   It makes you a Halloween cat.